BREAK MY FALL

Swoon Series

J.H. CROIX

This is a work of fiction. Names, characters, businesses, places, events and incidents are either the products of the author's imagination or used in a fictitious manner. Any resemblance to actual persons, living or dead, or actual events is purely coincidental.

Cover design by Najla Qamber Designs

Cover Photography: Wander Aguiar

Cover models: Shane MacKinnon & Adrea McNulty

❀ Created with Vellum

"Unless you love someone, nothing else makes sense." -E.E. Cummings

Sign up for my newsletter for information on new releases & get a FREE copy of one of my books!

http://jhcroixauthor.com/subscribe/

Follow me!

jhcroix@jhcroix.com
https://amazon.com/author/jhcroix
https://www.bookbub.com/authors/j-h-croix
https://www.facebook.com/jhcroix
https://www.instagram.com/jhcroix/

BREAK MY FALL

My rules: No players. No flirts. No cocky jerks.
My exception: Dawson Marsh.

Dawson might be every girl's crush in this small town, but not mine. I can appreciate him from a distance, and that suits me fine.

Except that one time he kissed me. Up close and personal.

Once is a mistake. But the second time? Sublime.

The man should come with some kind of a warning sign: Not safe for work! Hot to the touch! But what kind of girl can't handle a little friends with benefits action, right?

The one who missed the most important warning: Danger, risk of falling.

Chapter One

DAWSON

A waiter weaved through the crowd, carrying a tray of wine and beer. He paused beside me, and I snagged a pint of beer as the hum of conversation carried on around me. Usually, I was in my element like this. I could dive in, drink a little too much, party a little too hard, and flirt like there was no tomorrow. Preferably, a night like this would end with me in a warm and willing woman's bed.

Lately, I'd been clinging to the concept of "fake it until you make it."

An unmistakable voice drew my attention. "Oh my God!" Evie Blair exclaimed.

Following the sound, I saw Evie nudge some guy in the shoulder as he smiled down at her. By the angle of his eyes, I surmised he was catching a healthy glimpse of her cleavage. An entirely irrational streak of possessiveness jolted me. I didn't get possessive, much less jealous.

Shaking the feeling off, I took a moment to absorb her. Evie was lovely although not in any typical way. Oh, she had glossy dark hair that fell straight down her back and stunning rich blue eyes. I couldn't look into them for too long because it felt as if I were diving straight into the deep sea. I never knew if I'd be able to come up for air. With her slightly crooked nose, lopsided smile, and a dusting of freckles across the bridge of her nose, she was downright endearing. She was short with hips that swung with every step.

I dragged my eyes away from her, lifting my beer to my lips. I lowered it a second later and turned to set it on a counter along the wall behind me. I had no interest in drinking, and all my usual tricks were failing me.

"Hey, man," a voice said from over my shoulder.

Glancing to the side, I found Wade Ellis standing there. "Hey," I replied, forcing some semblance of a smile on my face.

"Not even drinking tonight?" he commented.

Shaking my head, I shrugged. "Nah. I'm here to support the lodge, but that's about it."

Lost Deer Winery, a premier winery in the Blue Ridge Mountains, was hosting a fundraiser for Stolen Hearts Rescue, an animal rescue program run by the same place where I worked.

I wasn't up for conversation, and blessedly, someone else said something to Wade, and he turned away to reply. Glancing at my watch, I calculated I'd been here for a solid hour, so more than enough time. If necessary, I would claim I had a headache. And in a way, I did.

Turning, I clapped Wade's shoulder as I passed by and started to weave through the crowd. I wasn't paying much attention to where I was going when Evie's voice caught my ears, dragging my gaze sideways to where she stood only a few feet away.

"Excuse me?" Her tone was sharp.

Without thinking, I veered closer, stopping at her side just as the man who had been staring down at her cleavage curled his hand around her upper arm. Her skin dimpled under his grip, deep enough I figured he'd leave bruises. I cut between them, shouldering the asshole out of the way.

The man's dark gaze swung to me, his mouth opening as if to protest. I glared at him, and he snapped his mouth shut. "What the fuck, dude?" he muttered as he released Evie's arm.

My eyes flicked down, noticing the red splotches left from his fingerprints on the soft curve of her bicep. "You okay?" I asked, glancing at Evie.

She looked up, a pink tinge cresting on her cheeks. "I'm fine." She looked back at the man. "Back the fuck off, asshole."

The guy simply snorted and shook his head before turning away. Another waiter walked past us just as a woman turned quickly. Her shoulder collided with the tray, sending three glasses of wine tipping to the side and splashing red wine all over Evie's dress.

"Gah!" Evie exclaimed, jumping back.

Evie didn't wear dresses too often. In fact, I didn't know if I'd ever seen her in one. The dress in question was a light, shimmery cream fabric. With a fitted bodice, it fell to her knees in a twirl, the sweet curve of her hips tempting me to run my hands over them. I didn't think it was meant to show off her curves, but with her, it was impossible for them not to show. She'd paired her dress with chunky black boots, which suited her perfectly.

Her dress was now stained red all over the front. Evie looked down and sighed, eyeing the wine stains running in streaks. With the waiter murmuring his apologies and the woman who'd run into the tray chiming in, Evie simply shrugged. "It happens. Leave it to me to take the wine tasting far more seriously than anyone else," she added with a laugh.

A genuine smile stretched across my face for what felt like the first time in weeks. Evie had that effect on me.

There was something so real about her it was hard not to smile.

The waiter interjected, "Ma'am, can I bring you a towel or anything?"

She shrugged. "Not much point to it. I guess I'll just cut out early." Her eyes scanned the room.

"Want a ride?" I asked.

I knew by chance she'd caught a ride here with Dani. Like me, Evie lived at Stolen Hearts Lodge where we both worked.

"You're leaving?" she countered, sounding surprised.

For a good reason. I wasn't usually wont to leave anything resembling a party early. I just couldn't find the mood for them over the past few weeks.

I met her gaze and nodded. "I was on my way out when I passed by."

"Okay." She glanced down at her wine-stained dress. "My dress is ruined."

I shrugged. "Maybe. Come on," I said, gesturing toward the exit at the back.

Evie fell into step beside me before stopping. "Wait a second. I need to let the girls know I'm leaving." She spun away, weaving through the crowd and ignoring the glances at her wine-stained dress. She stopped beside Shay and Dani, pointing at her dress and shaking her head. Shay's eyes met mine across the room, and I could sense her curiosity. I didn't usually leave early for anything.

Within a moment, Evie returned to my side. "Okay. Take me home."

Reflexively, I slipped my arm around her shoulders as we walked through the crowded winery. As soon as my hand landed on the curve of her shoulder, I became acutely aware of her silky skin. Her scent drifted to me, a hint of sugar and cream. I wanted to bury my nose in her hair. My hyper-awareness of her didn't make any sense. Or perhaps it did.

"Shay and Jackson are gonna make gobs of money for the rescue," Evie said just as we reached the door.

"I'll say, and that's a good thing. Jackson commented just last week that he's thinking of expanding the rescue program."

Her eyes canted up to mine as I held the door for her. "Really?" Answering her own question, she continued, "Well, it's full all the time anyway."

The door swung shut behind us as we stepped outside into the autumn air.

Fall in the Blue Ridge Mountains was definitely cooler than summer, a relief from the heat that hung over the landscape like a heavy curtain on the hottest days.

Our footsteps crunched as we walked across the gravel parking lot. I took a breath, feeling a subtle sense of ease inside. I hadn't felt like myself for going on a month. Just now, though, I felt a little lighter.

Evie didn't ask where my truck was and seemed content to follow me. I looked ahead. Lost Deer Winery sat on the hillside with a view out over Stolen Hearts Valley. The famous blue haze of the Blue Ridge Mountains was fading into the darkness, a mist shimmering above the mountain ridge in the distance.

The moon's silvery light cast everything in an ethereal glow. I took a deep breath, inhaling the air, earth scented from the fallen leaves.

"Where...?"

Evie's question trailed off when I slid my hand down her back, angling her with a gentle, coaxing pressure on her low back in the direction of my truck.

"Oh, there it is," she said brightly.

Out of habit, I went to the passenger's side and opened the door for her. Evie looked up at me, and I wanted to kiss her. With the moonlight on her hair, her eyes were a silvery blue, wide with surprise. "Well, geez, Dawson, I didn't know you could be a gentleman."

My laughter surprised me. Evie was easy to be with—so, so easy—and that was a gift.

"Amazing, isn't it?" I countered.

As a smile teased her lips, she climbed in, tucking her skirt carefully around her legs. With her smile buoying me, I closed the door and rounded the front of my truck, my body humming with anticipation. Evie's presence was a scattering of sparks on the fire banked between us. It had been there since I first met her.

Always.

I usually ignored it and deflected it with humor—because its potency frightened me a bit. With her haphazard beauty, her quirky personality, and her underlying sassy sweetness, she struck me as a woman who might not be satisfied with casual. As much as I wanted her, I hewed to what was safe so far.

During the drive, I felt her gaze on me and slid mine sideways when I came to a stop sign. In the dark cab of my truck, the air suddenly felt charged.

If only because Evie's presence had nudged me out of the edge of darkness where I'd been mentally teetering for weeks, I managed to tease. "Enjoying the view, are you?"

Her mouth dropped open. "Oh my God. You are *so* cocky," she said dryly. Her eyes were flashing, and I knew she enjoyed our banter as much as I did.

Looking away, I chuckled as I pressed my foot to the gas pedal, and the truck rolled forward. "I'm only cocky when it's obvious."

"What's obvious?"

"That you were enjoying the view. I wasn't gonna say anything about what the view might be. I don't have an opinion on that."

She burst out laughing, punching my shoulder lightly with her fist. "Let me guess. You rely on the women who throw themselves at your feet for an assessment of your looks?"

Sliding my gaze sideways again briefly, I winked before looking back at the road. "Oh no, I rely on the look in your eyes, sugar."

"Jesus, you are *too* much," she murmured. "How much longer is this drive?"

"Not much." I turned onto the road that led to Stolen Hearts Lodge.

"Thank God. Seriously, though, what gives?"

"What do you mean?"

"You leaving a party without a woman on your arm," she explained.

It was brief, but the sense of coldness that gusted through me was impossible to ignore. I shrugged, striving to keep my tone casual. "Nothing. Just tired. I am human, after all."

"Oh, and here I thought you were a vampire," she replied, her tone droll.

My laughter rumbled in my chest. Rolling to a stop, I parked in the area set aside for staff out behind the two renovated barns that comprised of the guest portion of the high-end adventure lodge where we worked. The parking lot was tucked in the trees, and several paths branched away from it, leading to the guest and staff cabins.

Evie was climbing out by the time I made it around the truck. I reached her just in time to catch her from stumbling. I had parked on the edge of the lot, and her boot slipped on the running board. My arm slipped around her waist as I commented, "Easy there."

A gasp slipped from her lips when she collided against me. Every soft inch of her. Despite working together for two years now, I had never been this close to Evie.

Her eyes swung up to mine. There was nothing but the hazy light of the moon to illuminate the deep blue of her gaze. My breath caught in my throat, and every cell in my body tightened. She was pressed against me. I could feel the tight points of her nipples through her dress.

I wasn't sure if she expected me to move away, but I couldn't seem to make myself do so. My eyes flicked down, snagging on her plush lips. The urge to kiss her was almost overwhelming.

Apparently, it *was* overwhelming. Before I was aware of what I was doing, I was dipping my head and brushing my lips across hers. They were soft and warm, and a little zing of electricity passed between us.

By the time my mind caught up to what was happening, I expected Evie to haul off and slap me, but she didn't. Instead, she let out a soft sigh and arched into me.

Just as I was about to fit my mouth over hers and dive in, I checked myself. With another brush of my lips over hers, I forced myself to lift my head. I couldn't step back just yet, though. She felt too good, and I was aroused as hell. I was certain she could feel my cock nestled at the apex of her thighs. Because somehow, we'd ended up plastered together when all I'd intended to do was help her out of the truck.

My heart was thrashing wildly in my chest, and the way I felt left me in shock. I felt more alive than I had in months, perhaps in years, and I didn't know what to do with any of it.

When I looked down, her eyes were closed, her dark lashes curled against her cheeks. I desperately wanted to know what she was thinking, and I just as urgently wanted to extricate myself from this situation.

Not because I wanted to be away from Evie. To the contrary. I wanted to carry her through the woods to my cabin, and that feeling was foreign to me. I enjoyed women, but I compartmentalized my enjoyment. It was nothing like this humming, driving need to claim her.

Her lashes swept up, her deep blue eyes locking with mine. My heart spun and stopped as though a compass finding its magnetic north.

Chapter Two

EVIE

Dawson Marsh was warm, tall, and strong. My pulse skittered out of control, and I could barely pull my thoughts together.

I was also annoyed as hell with myself. For two long years, even though I thought Dawson was oh, so tempting, I swore I would *not* fall for his charms. He was a master flirt and tease, and I didn't need that.

By some miracle, I managed to string together a few words. "What was that?"

When I looked up at Dawson, I expected to see his sly smirk. Instead, he looked as stunned as I felt.

"Hell if I know," he finally said, a wondering laugh slipping free.

That laugh pissed me right the hell off. Just what I needed.

I shimmied out from between the truck and where he stood, stalking away. "Thanks for the ride home," I called over my shoulder.

The sound of his truck door closing carried to me with his footsteps jogging across the gravel next. "Evie!" he called.

Turning, I watched as he approached me, stopping a few feet away, almost apprehensively.

"What?" I asked, resting a hand on my hip. I was relieved that it was mostly dark. My face was hot, and I didn't need this to get any worse with him noticing.

"I didn't mean to upset you."

"Have you been taken over by an alien?" I sputtered.

Dawson slipped his hands in his pockets, his lips kicking into a smile. "Not that I know of. You?"

"Definitely not. Anyway, let's forget that ever happened, okay?"

I didn't wait for his reply before I turned, striding quickly toward my cabin. I thought I heard him say something behind me and could've sworn it was, *What if I don't want to?*

I had no answer for that. Even the possibility of him saying that had flutters twirling in my belly, so I kept walking.

Letting myself into my cabin, I closed the door quietly, leaning against it and taking several deep breaths. Looking down, I sighed. I'd completely forgotten why I left the fundraiser early. My pretty new dress was ruined. Red wine had dried in a giant splotch smack in the middle of my chest with streaks running all the way to the hem.

"Fuck," I muttered.

I kicked off my boots, the hardwood floor cool under my feet as I strolled across the room and into the bathroom. I faced the full-length mirror mounted on the wall by the shower and frowned. I looked like I'd partied hard and straggled home. Walking closer to the mirror, I took stock.

Unconsciously, I pressed my fingers against my lips. They were still tingling from Dawson's kiss.

"I don't know if it counts as a kiss," I said aloud to myself.

Well, what else is it called when two people's lips press together? My internal snark snapped right back.

"Fine, it was kind of a kiss."

Although I certainly thought Dawson was handsome—who wouldn't?—I knew I wasn't his type. I'd seen his type. Dawson liked to play the field. He was quite shameless about it, in fact.

He liked his women willowy and classically beautiful, preferably not expecting a damn thing from him. Definitely not thin, I had curves aplenty. I gave my plump ass a little smack.

I wasn't ashamed of my body, but I was realistic, brutally realistic. My dark hair was straight and usually in a ponytail. I'd worn it down tonight for all the good that did. The only man who noticed me had been a total ass.

Lifting my arm, I eyed the bruises forming where that ass had grabbed me. He startled me so much, I didn't even remember what I said that set him off. I could be flippant and probably said something that annoyed him.

Dawson's presence had been a relief when he cut in like he was some kind of a protector of mine. My confusion about Dawson only spun tighter the more I thought about our kiss. We were friends and had an ongoing teasing relationship. But I'd made myself a promise it wouldn't go any further.

I could be epically stupid when it came to men. With a sigh, I turned away from the mirror to peel out of my ruined dress and toss it in the laundry basket. I couldn't quite bring myself to throw it away just yet. Maybe Dani knew some trick to get that god-awful stain out.

A hot shower later, I toweled off and put on my most comfortable pair of flannel jammies. When Dawson strolled into my thoughts, I kicked him out. Again. But I couldn't stop thinking of what couldn't have been more than one minute between us. The feel of his hard body and the brush of his lips on mine were branded in my memory.

Sleep teased me for most of the night with Dawson filling my thoughts despite my protests.

"Here you go," I said, deftly placing a plate on the table. I was serving a group of college guys at the lodge restaurant.

As I set down the next plate, the guy glanced up at me and winked. "Thanks, sweetheart. Don't suppose you can join us for drinks later?" he asked.

Despite his teasing tone, I suspected he was quite confident I would preen under the compliment contained within his request.

The guy in question appeared to have forgotten I knew who he was. Johnny Simpson and I actually went to high school together. He ignored me most of the time back then. Well, except for when he went along with one of his entourage girls when they teased me. Because he was *that* guy—the one who had girls trailing him in the halls.

I smiled tightly, not caring to refresh his memory. "No, thanks. Anything else I can get for you guys?" I asked as I slid the last plate onto the table.

"I'm all set," one of the guys said.

Johnny appeared to be about to reply to my dismissal, but another customer nearby conveniently saved me when a man raised his empty coffee mug. Casting a quick smile around the table, I added, "Just let me know if you need anything else. I'll check back shortly."

Spinning away, I continued with my shift. It was busy tonight at Stolen Hearts Lodge, but I preferred it that way. The tips tended to be generous here, and I didn't like to stare at the clock.

Unfortunately for me, Johnny didn't give up his flirting. After his group departed, he waited by the table, standing with his thumb pressing the credit card tightly against the bill tray. With his friends gone, I was stuck dealing with him without an audience.

"Now, I hate when a girl says no," he said with what I thought was an attempt at a charming smile.

I decided Dani Love, my boss and friend, would probably forgive me for what I was about to say. "Johnny Simpson, are you going to hold that bill hostage until I agree to have drinks with you?"

A look of surprise flitted across his face. "You know who I am?" he asked, his tone only slightly cooler, still cajoling and still paired with that fake charming smile.

"We went to high school together, Johnny. I'm Evie Blair," I said, my tone short.

It took him a few seconds, and then his eyes widened. "Evie Blair?"

I ignored the flash of embarrassment likely creeping up my cheeks. High school sucked for me. I was awkward with nothing quite fitting together on my face. I also had the worst summer of my life the year before ninth grade. My twin sister died, and I felt as if half of me had literally died with her.

Blessedly, I had a supportive family, but high school was what it was, and it'd been miserable.

Johnny didn't seem to pick up on any cues, a slight gleam entering his gaze. "Well damn, Evie, you sure have grown up."

I eyed him for a long moment. "Pay your fucking bill, Johnny. There's no chance in hell I'm going anywhere with you. You were an asshole in high school, and maybe you've changed, but somehow, I doubt it."

"Okay, okay," he drawled. "When have I ever been an asshole?"

I stared at him, resting a hand on my hip. "Maybe the time you laughed when one of your girlfriends dumped her drink over my head. Or perhaps when another one teased me because my twin sister died? Which one was it? I can't recall, but maybe you can."

For a moment, I thought he experienced a hint of guilt. Then he laughed. "Don't be so uptight." He tossed the bill tray on the table and walked out, sliding his credit card into his wallet. Yeah, he was that kind of asshole. He was going to leave without bothering to pay the bill. All because I hadn't given him what he wanted.

My chest was hot, and my skin felt tight. Turning, I scanned the restaurant wildly. I found Dani a few tables away, quietly loading the remnants of a finished dinner and dirty plates on a tray.

I approached her, the empty tray in my hand hanging at my side. "Hey Dani, let me..." I began to say, but she looked up and shook her head.

"No need to apologize. Johnny Simpson's always been an asshole. Now I have a good reason to turn him away the next time he shows up."

Dani had been a few years ahead of me in high school, just like Johnny. I met her eyes, the tension bundled in my chest easing quickly. "Thanks, Dani. In case I forgot to say it this week, you're the best boss ever."

Dani smiled, lifting the full tray of dishes from the table and nudging her chin over to the table where Johnny and his friends had been. "Clean that table. Let's finish tonight." At the last minute before she turned away, she glanced back at me. "I just hate assholes."

I did too. But then, not everyone learned the painful lessons of high school when you didn't quite fit in. I'd gained plenty of confidence since then and enjoyed flirting and teasing just as much as anyone else. Confidence aside, I didn't think I would ever enjoy the company of men like Johnny.

As I gathered the plates from the table, Dawson strolled into my thoughts. He was nothing like Johnny. In fact, I couldn't imagine him standing by when someone was cruel to anyone for any reason. He was a tease, but he was always kindhearted and harmless.

Yet I didn't doubt for a second that Dawson had been at the top of the social heap in high school. He hadn't grown up around Stolen Hearts Valley. He was from some town on the coast of North Carolina. No doubt, he'd been a surfer. With his easy looks and quick charm, he probably had his own entourage of girls hanging on his every word back then.

He certainly did now when he hit the town. With a mental eye roll, I reminded myself that was why it was crazy for me to think he liked me. It didn't matter that the brief brush of his lips against mine had sent a thrill through my body and still made my lips tingle whenever I thought about it.

Chapter Three

DAWSON

I leaned against the bar at Lost Deer Bar, catching the bartender's eye. "House draft," I called when she looked my way.

I'd done my share of flirting with Delilah Carter, but that was all it had ever been. I would even admit I actually tried to take her home one night. Rather, I tried to persuade her to take me home. I didn't take women home with me. That sent too many mixed messages.

Delilah had flicked her ponytail over her shoulder and rolled her eyes so hard they almost fell out of her head. She'd told me she had more than enough men to flirt with her, and she certainly didn't need a one-night stand. We'd been friends ever since.

Delilah rested her hips against the cooler as she slid the pint of beer across the glossy wood bar to me. "Here you go, hot stuff. Haven't seen you in here as much the past few weeks. What gives?" she asked.

I took a sip of my beer before replying. The thing was, I didn't care to explain. A familiar cloud that came along every so often had settled over me, and I couldn't seem to shake it with my usual tricks. After a moment, I shrugged. "Just busy as hell. Work, life, and all that jazz. Miss me?" I attempted to tease, but I knew it was weak.

Delilah smiled. "Of course. Without you here, that's one less person I can give a hard time. You, my man, know how to roll with it. I'm not the only one who's noticed your absence. Rumors are starting to circulate that you might've gotten serious with someone, though no one seems to know who the hell with. I even considered hitting Dani up for gossip, but I thought that might piss you off."

I laughed and rolled my eyes. "No, I'm not serious with anyone. Although I don't doubt Dani would know if I was."

Delilah flashed me a smile and a wink before turning away to deal with a customer at the other end of the bar. Sliding my hips onto a barstool in the corner, I cast my gaze about the room. Delilah's observation was pointed. I hadn't been here much lately and wasn't even sure I wanted to be here tonight. I had talked myself into the mental equivalent of a jumpstart on my brain. Whether I wanted to or not, I was determined to have a few beers and go home with someone.

Don't go thinking I was the worst sort of player. I really wasn't. I was more for flirting and having fun and keeping things light than anything else. Oh sure, I had my share of casual hookups, but not as often as people thought. I didn't bother to correct impressions people formed over nothing more than seeing me flirt.

An hour later, I was still only halfway through my first beer. Despite more than one woman stopping to say hello and attempting to start a teasing conversation that just might go somewhere, I wasn't feeling it. At all.

"Fuck my life," I muttered. I tossed a few bills in Delilah's tip jar and threw her a quick wave as I turned to leave. I left my half-empty beer on the bar behind me.

It was a clear night, and the stars glittered in the darkness. As I looked up into the sky, idly counting the stars, I took a breath and let it out slowly. The air held only a hint of the cool autumn to come. After another breath, I walked to my truck. Although my attempt to reset and fall into my usual escape of a few drinks, flirting, and fun had failed, I had a backup to try to get my bearings.

After parking my truck at the lodge, the leaves and pine needles crunched under my boots as I followed the path through the trees. As I veered off the main path and up an incline, I was relieved the half-moon cast just enough of a glow that I could keep my footing in the darkness.

Moments later, after startling a deer and hearing a bat flying above as I walked, the trees opened up, and the ground leveled out again. The large rock here was nature's way of offering a seat for a good view. I settled my hips on the cool surface with my feet just resting on the ground. The lights of downtown Stolen Hearts Valley were visible from here, illuminating the town's shape.

Leaning back, I rested my hands under my head and stared at the bright stars in the sky. My mind skipped back to a month ago. As a first responder for Stolen Hearts Valley, I'd been on call. I'd responded with Jackson and a crew to a home. The unconscious man's face loomed large in my memory, along with the pills scattered on the floor beside him. The team worked fast, and he survived.

I could still hear the rush of his breath when he came to, and the look in his eyes had haunted me ever since. I didn't know if it was relief or disappointment.

I recognized the wish to just let it all go. When depression rolled over me, it was like a weighted mist. My psyche couldn't breathe very well, and I felt cold inside, so fucking cold. I didn't want to give in. Ever. I got tired of how depression came back and claimed me. A few years of therapy in college had helped, yet sometimes, being clear-eyed and accepting what was happening sucked.

I'd had more than one therapist give me quite the look when I was honest about the fact that partying helped.

What they didn't get was I wasn't really ever out of control. All I needed was to take the edge off. I never took it too far.

"Dawson?" A voice came through the darkness, soft with a distinctive rasp to it. As far as I knew, Evie didn't smoke, but she still had a voice like a jazz singer in a smoky bar. It was sexy as hell.

My chest tightened. I didn't want her to see me like this. But I had nowhere to hide, and no one else was around.

Man up and deal with her, my weary but strong side said.

I didn't even bother to sit up. "Hey, Evie," I called into the night.

The leaves rustled under her feet as she approached. She stopped beside the rock.

"Are you okay?" she asked, the concern clear in her voice.

Considering it was dark, I had no idea how she could sense I wasn't doing so great. Fucking shitty much was the truth, but I didn't feel like talking about that just now. Somehow, Evie's simple concern was like a sliver of sunlight in a shadowy room.

I rolled up to a seated position and managed a genuine smile. "I've been better, but I'm okay."

"You found my spot," she announced.

"Your spot?"

With nothing but the moonlight illuminating her face, I could barely see the subtle flush crest on her cheeks. She turned and shimmied her hips onto the rock beside me.

I hadn't seen her since that kiss. I didn't like to contemplate, but I'd thought about it far too much. Glancing at her profile in the darkness, I added, "I thought this was my spot."

Evie swung her feet, the heels of her tennis shoes bumping against the side of the rock, the sound soft in the darkness. "I guess it's our rock then. Whenever I've come before, nobody else has ever been here. I thought of it as mine, but I don't mind sharing," she offered generously.

That ray of sunshine widened as though the shade on a

window had opened and cast a soft light over me. I chuckled. "Why, thank you."

She leaned her head back to look up at the stars, and I found myself following her gaze, wondering how she saw the night sky.

"The Little Dipper is my favorite," she said.

"Yeah? How come?"

"Because it doesn't take up too much space, and it's so cute."

Another laugh threatened to break loose, and I didn't hold it back. "I suppose that's as good a reason as any."

"Do you have a favorite?"

Scanning the sky, I offered, "Orion. It's usually visible from early winter to spring."

"Oh, I like that one too. I like them all really. I have a telescope in my cabin."

Bringing my gaze down and sliding it sideways to her, I asked, "You do?"

Her eyes met mine, the blue somehow bright in the moonlight. "I do. Sometime, if you want, I'll bring it up here."

"I'd like that," I heard myself saying.

Evie smiled and looked forward again. We sat quietly for several minutes, but it was a comfortable silence. As much as I teased Evie, it was partly because I was comfortable with her. Oh, and perhaps because I liked her. I was so in the habit of using jokes and humor to ease the darkness inside that sometimes claimed me that I lost sight of some things occasionally.

For example, when I teased Evie, it wasn't to escape. I was like a little boy in grade school tugging on pigtails because he liked a girl and didn't know how to tell her.

Evie spoke again, nudging me out of my thoughts. "Why do you come up here?"

With the darkness to cloak us and the way I felt with her, I found myself being far less dismissive and more honest than I would normally be. Not that I was purposely dishonest—because that wasn't quite how it was—but it was more that I sidestepped things. A good laugh was a quick way to distract someone.

Yet just now, I didn't do that with her. "I like coming here. It's peaceful, and it's quiet no matter what time of day it is. I can clear my head. How about you?"

When I looked in her direction, she had caught her bottom lip in her teeth and was nibbling on it. Nothing about these moments with her made any sense, so the fact that my cock twitched at the sight of that didn't faze me any more than the rest. She was beautiful, damn beautiful, and my reaction to her had always been swift, fierce, and instantaneous. To the point that it frightened me slightly, which was why I usually teased her and avoided getting too close.

Danger, danger was what my mind should've been saying. Yet it wasn't.

She turned to look at me. When I glimpsed the pain contained in her eyes, I suddenly wanted to hold her close and do anything to erase whatever caused her to hurt.

"I come here when I miss my twin sister."

It was her pain, but simply hearing it felt like a knife sliding across the surface of my heart, the cut sharp and deep. "I'm sorry," I said. Sorry didn't seem sufficient, but I had no idea what else to say.

I felt more than saw the twist of her mouth. "I'd say it's okay, but it's not really. Thank you."

"I didn't know you had a twin sister."

"Yeah, you didn't grow up around here, so I don't see how you would know. Krista died in a boating accident. It's been twelve years, so I guess I've gotten used to her being gone, but I don't think I'll ever stop missing her. I like the quiet here too. I don't mean to sound weird, but I guess it surprises me you need somewhere to clear your head. What's that about?"

Taking a breath, I let it out slowly. Evie had been honest

about a brutal loss, so I felt I owed her the same level of honesty. "Nothing particularly specific, just that sometimes I get a little down, and I need to stop thinking so hard."

For a moment, I saw surprise flit through her gaze. I thought maybe she would tease me and braced myself for it, but she didn't.

"It's a good place for that," she said softly. Before I realized what she was about to do, she reached over and curled her hand over mine where it rested on the rock between us, squeezing it as if to comfort me.

"Now you seem like you might be worrying about me, Evie, when here I am worrying about you," I said, ignoring the slight hitch in my voice.

"We can worry about each other. That's what friends are for, right?"

"Are we friends then?"

"Of course. You might play silly practical jokes on me, but I consider you a friend, Dawson."

"Damn, girl"—I thumped my fist on my chest over my heart—"you can actually get to me."

Evie's laughter rang out in the darkness, and she squeezed my hand tighter. Somehow, she'd lightened the moment perfectly.

Chapter Four

DAWSON

I didn't want to let go of Evie's hand. I wanted to stay right here with her. With some special magic, she had helped to dissipate that cloud rolling over me. And not because she distracted me—okay, she did distract me, but not in *that* way right this moment—but because of just the way she was so matter of fact, so genuine even when it might hurt.

Once again, we fell into a comfortable silence, this time with her hand warm in mine. Because I was me, and I wasn't accustomed to letting myself experience anything this real, a thread of anxiety started to spool tightly inside. I was close personal friends with depression and anxiety. I'd learned they often came to see me hand in hand, taking turns testing my ability to withstand them.

Restless and not wanting to ruin this moment, I decided departing from it was better than letting those feelings take over. Squeezing her hand before releasing it, I slipped my hips off the rock and turned to face her.

"I'll let you have the rock to yourself now."

I was no more than a foot away from her when she looked up at me. As if lightning flashed from the sky in the darkness, the air around us electrified suddenly. My feet were rooted to the ground as the sensation spun around me.

Evie stared up at me. The sound of her breath catching in her throat was audible in the quiet. Without thinking, I closed the distance between us, stepping between her knees and lifting a hand to trail my fingers through the ends of her hair.

The moment felt suspended in time with the air shimmering around us and a sense of intimacy twining like a vine with desire. I found myself dipping my head and brushing my lips across hers. She sighed, the sound of her breath tugging at my heart.

I stepped a little closer, my knees bumping against the rock as I slid a hand through her hair, lightly cupping the nape of her neck and angling her head to deepen our kiss. She gasped when I swept my hand down her back and slipped my tongue inside her mouth to glide against hers.

I had kissed my share of women. Frankly, I wasn't much of a fan of kissing. In fact, I usually avoided it. It felt too intimate.

Nothing with Evie fit into any pattern I'd ever had. I couldn't imagine *not* kissing her. It was so fucking hot—the soft sounds that came from the back of her throat were little lashes of a whip against the lust driving me, and the way her plush lips were mobile under mine drew me in deeper by the millisecond.

Her body was warm and lush with her breasts pressed against my chest. I could feel her nipples, and I knew she could feel my arousal. I hadn't planned it that way, but my cock was notched right against her core.

Part of me wanted to simply let loose into this. The pulse of desire beat wildly between us. It was so fucking good. I'd never experienced anything even close to this intensity. Another part of me spoke louder. I didn't want to ruin this or make it something it wasn't. I knew by rushing that was exactly what I would do.

This kiss—which could last forever as far as I was concerned—was fucking heaven. It fed a part of my soul I hadn't even known existed—the part that craved something raw, something authentic and intimate.

I felt the press of Evie's hand against my back, her touch a light brand. She broke free of our kiss and gulped in air.

I did the same. For the first time in my life, I was breathless. From nothing more than a kiss. A hot kiss, but still just a kiss.

We stared at each other. I could barely see her in the darkness, but I could make out the blue of her eyes and feel the pounding of her heartbeat against mine.

"What was that?" she asked, her words falling quietly between us.

My heart tumbled in my chest. Taking a breath, I replied, "A kiss."

Evie's laugh was soft. "Well, I know that, Dawson."

I could feel her gaze searching my face, and I suddenly wanted to turn away. As comfortable as it was to be with her, the desire I felt for her was disorienting in its power.

"Come on," I said, starting to turn away, "I'll walk you back."

Her hand caught mine, stopping me in my tracks. Her touch was light. "Dawson."

Turning back, I faced her again, my heart beating so hard I could hear its force echoing in my ears. "What?"

"What's with kissing me? That's twice now."

If only she could see the thoughts spinning wheelies in my mind. I wanted to say, *Because I like you, because you're beautiful, because you're funny, because you're the only person in the world I feel this way with, because maybe I want something other than a one-night stand.*

I might not have had a ton of experience with relationships, but I knew quite well if I said any of those things at this moment, it would freak the hell out of Evie. It sure as hell freaked me out. I tried to call upon the part of myself that was quick with a joke and could make light of just about any moment. But I couldn't.

So perhaps I didn't say my crazy string of thoughts aloud, but I was honest. "I don't know. I've wanted to kiss you for a long time."

When I heard the hiss of her breath, I almost laughed because I knew I had startled her.

She shimmied her hips off the rock, the sound of her feet crunching in the leaves as she stood beside me. I sensed she didn't quite know what to think.

My mouth, meanwhile, apparently had more to say. "Maybe you haven't thought about it much, but I don't think there's much sense in arguing that something's there."

She stayed silent as we turned and began walking through the trees together. Although I was a bit stunned with myself, I was strangely at peace. I'd simply been direct, and that was all I could do.

"Well, I mean, no, I won't argue there's nothing there," she eventually murmured. "But I don't think I'm quite your type."

"I don't have a type. And being totally honest, that was the hottest kiss I've ever had, so I guess you're my type."

She stumbled, and I caught her by the elbow to steady her.

"Are you serious?" she asked, her tone disbelieving. "I'm not anything like the women you usually go for."

It hurt, and I couldn't believe it did, but I was getting the idea she had written me off. I supposed I deserved it. I was the one who was committed to no-strings sex. I was the one who didn't bother to correct assumptions. I certainly didn't have as much sex as people thought I did, but I kept busy.

"Think what you want," I finally replied, turning with her when she resumed walking.

I didn't want to let go of her, so I slid my hand down her arm and caught hers in mine. For just a moment, she tensed, but then she laced her fingers through mine. After a few minutes, we reached the main path, and I reluctantly let go of her hand when she gave it a little tug.

"I can walk the rest of the way," she said, looking up at me. I could see her better now because lights were strung through the trees here. By chance, her cabin was in one direction and mine in the other.

"I'll walk you," I replied.

"You're such a man," she muttered under her breath as she fell into step beside me.

"Well, seeing as I *am* a man, I won't argue the point."

Evie laughed. "Fine."

When we reached her cabin, I paused at the base of the steps. She stopped one step above me and turned back. For a moment, I thought she was going to say something else and revisit our conversation from moments ago. But she didn't. After a considering look, all she said was, "Thanks, Dawson. I'm sure I'll see you tomorrow."

With emotion spinning inside me, I nodded. "Good night," I called right before she closed the door.

Sleep came more easily than it had in weeks, that little ray of sun cast through the room of my life breaking through the darkness that had threatened to descend. Which was a miracle, given how unsettled I'd felt after Evie's comment that she wasn't my type.

Evie might not believe me, but I was going to prove her wrong.

Chapter Five

EVIE

"Here's your change," Nancy said as she handed over a few bills.

I stuffed them in the tip cup on the counter at Wake & Bake Café, smiling over at her. "Thanks!" Pausing to sip my coffee, I sighed. "The best."

Nancy chuckled, shooing me away with her hand. "Grab a table, hon. I've got more customers behind you."

With an apologetic smile cast their way, I crossed over to snag a small round table by the front windows that looked out over Main Street in downtown Stolen Hearts Valley. I took several sips of my coffee, savoring the rich, dark flavor and the caffeine. I let my eyes coast over the space. In a renovated old home with a bright blue roof, wide plank hardwood flooring, and tall windows, the space was warm and welcoming. They served the usual fare for a coffee shop but also lunch and an early dinner. I loved coming here when I had the time.

My mind spun back to several nights prior. I still didn't know what to think of Dawson kissing me. My body could *not* forget it. Every single time I thought about it—which, if

I was honest, was almost every hour—I got a fluttery feeling in my belly and heat spiraled through me.

After surviving my awkward adolescence, I'd managed to date a little but not much. I had a few short-lived relationships in college and realized the casual hookup scene wasn't my thing.

So whatever Dawson wanted from me, I was quite certain it wasn't a good idea for my sanity. Maybe we had chemistry, considering nothing more than a kiss from him left me more stirred up than any other encounter I'd ever had, but it wasn't smart. Not for me.

Dawson took the concept of being a player to heart. He took it so much to heart that the guys around the lodge teased him about never bringing anyone back to his bed. According to Wade, Dawson viewed that as too much of a commitment.

I would just have to convince my body not to like him so much. I would also have to convince myself not to let my heart think I might've seen another side of him.

Mentally ordering myself to stop thinking about him, I stared out the window. Downtown Stolen Hearts Valley was a lovely little town nestled in the Blue Ridge Mountains. These were the kind of mountains that felt like they were giving you a hug. With nooks and crannies, rich greenery, and the blue haze making an appearance regularly, I loved it here.

The sun was still rising, the sky a mix of a silvery gray-blue haze shot through with the gold of the morning sun. The rays were strengthening as the sun came to vanquish the darkness with day.

"Well, mornin', Evie."

The moment I heard Dawson's voice, a shiver rippled through me. This was going to get inconvenient *real* fast. I might've crushed on Dawson before, but it was just an appreciation of how hot he was with his shaggy blond hair and those dangerous silver-gray eyes.

He just had to go and kiss me. *Twice*. Taking a deep breath, I glanced over my shoulder to find him stopping beside the table.

Those eyes? Oh, God, those eyes. The moment my gaze collided with his, heat flashed through me, causing my skin to prickle all over.

"Good morning, Dawson," I said politely, hoping the flush I felt steaming through me didn't show on my face.

I wanted to play it cool and calm, but I'd never been good at that. Even though I was no longer an awkward teenage girl, my lingering insecurities clung to me, and guys like Dawson always set them off.

I took a quick sip of my coffee, swallowing too fast and choking on it. Sputtering, I snagged a napkin from the stack tucked between the cream and sugar by the window. Then, I just had to try to look at him and catch my breath too soon, only to start coughing all over again.

"Hey there, you okay?" he asked, his gaze concerned as one of his hands fell to the center of my back and moved in a soothing circle.

Great, just great. Dawson was now comforting me as I had a coughing fit all because I looked at him.

"I'm fine," I managed after a moment. I hated my body's traitorous response to him. His touch felt so good I wanted to purr like a cat.

It's just been too long since you've had sex, my sly mind said. True, so true.

To be specific, it had been almost two years. Long enough that I commiserated with Grace the other night and wondered if I was getting too out of practice. She'd commiserated right along with me.

"Mind if I join you?" he asked once I was breathing normally. Without waiting for my reply, he slipped into the chair directly across from me.

My feisty side finally kicked into gear. The coughing fit

over, I cocked my head to the side. "Well, now that you're sitting, I'll look mighty cranky if I say no."

Dawson's slow smile sent my belly into a series of flips. Almost as if it were trying to show off for him with a personal gymnastics routine.

His gray eyes crinkled at the corners. His blond hair was dark and still damp from a shower, I presumed. Seeing as it was only six in the morning, I gathered he'd come straight here from the lodge.

"Skipping out on breakfast with the crew?" I asked.

Dawson shook his head. "Of course not. I'll have coffee here and head back just in time for whatever Dani's making for everyone this morning. I wouldn't miss her food for anything. Are you skipping out on breakfast?" He clucked, shaking his head. "Who's going to tell Dani?"

"She knows I like to come here a few times a week. Since I work in the restaurant, I'm always scarfing on things."

Dawson grinned. "Of course."

Nancy paused at our table, asking, "Need anything, Dawson?"

"A coffee, darlin'," he replied swiftly.

She rolled her eyes as she passed by, giving his shoulder a pat. "You are too charming for your own good. I'll be right back with that coffee."

Dawson winked. Although I knew that certainly wasn't his point, his ease with flirting and teasing was a fresh reminder of why I needed to keep him at a distance. Hot kisses aside, I didn't need to be another one of Dawson's playthings.

He turned his attention back to me. I felt as if he were assessing me, trying to see all my secrets. I took another sip of my coffee, managing not to choke on it this time. I counted that as a win.

"What?" I finally asked, resisting the urge to squirm under his appraisal.

"I was just wondering how to change your mind."

"Huh? Change my mind about what?"

"You said you're not my type, and I disagree."

I sputtered on a swallow of coffee.

His silver-gray gaze darkened, and I felt a tug low in my belly. Just when I was about to reply after a fortifying sip of my coffee, Nancy arrived at our table again.

"Here you go, black and strong just like you like it. Anything else?" she asked, glancing back and forth between us.

"I'm all set, thanks."

Dawson nodded with me. "Same here. Thank you. I'll pay on the way out."

"Of course, you will. If you forget, I know you'll be back." She winked and hurried off.

During that brief exchange, I kind of hoped Dawson would forget what he just said, but no such luck. His gaze swung back to me. He had absolutely zero trouble with direct eye contact. I imagined that was one of his charms for any woman who was after the no-strings fun he offered.

With his eyes on me, I felt as if I were the only woman in the world at that moment. It felt as if we were in the middle of nowhere all by ourselves, so intent was his attention.

"You were saying?" he prompted before pausing to take a sip of his coffee.

I sighed. So much for avoidance. "I didn't say anything. But, face it, you like your women beautiful and casual. I'm neither."

His eyes narrowed. "Evie, that's bullshit. You're ..."

I shook my head, suddenly feeling rather fierce about clarifying. "For starters, we work together. It's a bad idea to get tangled up. We're practically neighbors. And ..." I had to pause for another sip of coffee. "I don't really do the casual thing like you."

For a flash, I thought I might've seen a hint of pain in his gaze, but it disappeared as quickly as I must've imagined it. He stayed quiet for a few beats, and then said, "That kiss was the hottest kiss I've ever had. And it was just a kiss. Plus, I don't just want something casual with you."

When my mouth fell open, his lips curled in a rueful smile. "I get it. Let me take you to dinner."

I almost choked on my coffee—again!—and glared at him when he started to laugh. "What?" I finally managed to sputter.

"Just what I said. Let me take you out to dinner."

Staring into his silvery-gray eyes, I gave my head a little shake. "Dawson, that's crazy. Did you hear my point about us working together?"

He was quiet, the teasing gleam fading from his eyes. His shoulders rose and fell with a breath, and he shrugged. "That part's not a big deal. I'm not your boss, and you're just trying to find an excuse. I didn't think it was that crazy, but obviously, you disagree."

I sensed I had actually hurt Dawson's feelings, but I was floundering inside and thrown off balance. When I opened my mouth to say something, though I didn't know what I was going to say, his phone chirped loudly.

Slipping it out of the pocket of his jeans, he glanced at the screen. As he looked back at me, his mouth kicked into a wry smile. "Saved by the bell. I gotta take this. We have a call."

Standing with his coffee in hand, he looked down at me once more, his gaze considering. Whatever he meant to say, it appeared he thought better of it. "Catch you later," he said as he turned away, pausing briefly at the counter to pay before striding out.

My eyes tracked him as he left. He moved with a lithe grace, his muscled form rangy and powerful. Of course, I couldn't help but linger for a moment on his fine ass. Dear God. He just had to go and make jeans look awesome.

I wasn't entirely conscious of just how hard I stared until Grace's voice broke through. "Well, gee, make sure you get a good enough look."

My cheeks were hot as I jerked my eyes away from him when he reached the door. Looking up at Grace, I shrugged. “You have to admit he’s got a nice ass.”

Grace laughed as she slipped into the chair across from me, occupying the seat Dawson left behind. “I will admit Dawson has a nice ass. I didn’t know you were so interested in it, though. What were you two talking about anyway? Dawson looked kind of serious.”

Grace was my best friend, and before my twin sister died, she’d been close to both of us. She’d been there at a time when I didn’t feel like I had many friends after Krista died.

I met her eyes and shrugged. “I think I’ve entered an alternate universe. He just asked me out to dinner.”

“What?” Grace asked, her eyebrows hitching up so high they almost hit her hairline.

“Exactly what I said. I guess I should fill in a few blanks. He kissed me the other night, and then once before that.”

“You have *so* been holding out on me,” she said, leaning back in her chair and taking a long sip of her coffee. Circling her hand in the air, she arched a brow, clearly expecting me to continue.

“Grace, I don’t have any idea what to say. Here’s what happened. Remember the fundraiser thing at Lost Deer Winery last week?” At her nod, I continued, “Well, he gave me a ride home after I got wine all over my dress. Which, by some miracle, Dani got out. Anyway, when he was helping me out of the truck, he kissed me. It was just a barely there thing, but it definitely was a kiss. I was totally freaked out and pretty much ran away from him. Then, the other night, I went up to that rock, and he was there. It’s kind of weird. For once, he wasn’t just giving me crap, and then he kissed me, like *really* kissed me.”

My cheeks got hot all over again just thinking about it.

Grace was quiet, her eyes a little wide. “Well, based on the look on your face, I’m guessing it was a good kiss.”

“Not my point.” I rolled my eyes. “I’m serious. I don’t

know what to think of any of this. A little advice would be helpful."

Grace sobered. "I don't know what to say. It was always obvious to me he had a thing for you. Did y'all plan this coffee date?"

Shaking my head, I took a sip of my coffee before replying. "No. I was already here, and then he showed up."

"And said he wanted to take you to dinner?" she prompted.

"Uh-huh."

"What did you say?"

"I told him it was crazy. To make it even crazier, I'm pretty sure I hurt his feelings. Then he got a call for the first responder team and said he had to go," I explained, gesturing to the door.

Grace picked up a fork, flipping it back and forth between her fingers. "Maybe he really likes you. I would imagine playing the field would get old eventually, even for him."

"That's the thing. I can't do that. It will be a mess."

She shrugged. "Maybe, maybe not. With the way you were staring at his ass, my guess is you might want to see how things play out. Or just tell him that it needs to be ... Oh, I don't know what the hell I'm talking about," she said with a sigh.

"Thanks for the advice," I offered.

Grace chewed on the inside of her cheek. "Sorry I'm not more help. I don't really know what to tell you. Dawson is totally cute, and it's obvious you two kind of have a buzz."

"A buzz? What do you mean?"

"Okay, Dawson teases everyone, like everyone. But it's different with you, and the way you react is different. That's all I'm saying. I guess you should just think about what you want. If anything. You did complain you haven't had sex in forever," she said, a sly grin stretching across her face. "According to the rumors, Dawson is, uh, magic in bed."

"See!" I threw my hands up in the air in exasperation. "That's why I can't be added to his list."

"List?"

"The only reason you hear rumors about what he's like in bed is because he's busy."

Grace rolled her eyes. "What's wrong with good sex? I could use some too. Don't go thinking I want it with Dawson because I don't. Since you do, maybe you should do something about it," she said with a giggle.

I glared at her.

Her smile faded. "Seriously, though, maybe Dawson does like no-strings sex, and there's nothing wrong with that. He's not an asshole about it, and he doesn't play people against each other, which is a lot more than I can say for others."

"I know. John was such a dick to you. I'm glad you're over him," I said, referencing a guy she dated over a year ago. She found out he wasn't exclusive although he'd led her to think he was and then tried to make her jealous with a now-former friend from college.

"Oh, I most definitely am, but it still totally sucked."

"The right guy will come along. I just know it."

I opened my mouth to say something, and Grace shook her head. "Don't."

"Grace, I wasn't going to tease."

"I know. It's just that's the past, and it needs to stay in the past."

"Okay, fine."

Although we weren't speaking his name, we were referring to Grace's high school boyfriend. Boone Reeves had moved back to town a few months ago and taken a position with Stolen Hearts Valley Emergency Response. While he wasn't working at the lodge, his connections with too many shared friends who did was too close for comfort for Grace. I had teased her a little at first, unaware of how thoroughly he had broken her heart. I wasn't that shitty of a best friend, but Grace hadn't given me all the details of what happened when she'd been away at college.

After glancing at my watch, I looked back at her. "Thanks for listening, even if you don't know what to tell me about Dawson."

Grace grinned. "Always. What time is your shift today?"

"In a half hour. I should get going. You headed back?"

"Not yet. I need to take care of a few errands. Need anything from the grocery store?"

"I don't think so. Oh wait, get me some coffee, would you?"

"Sure thing. I'll drop it off at your cabin this afternoon."

I departed Wake & Bake Café with a wave to Nancy behind the counter. Once I got to work in the lodge restaurant, my morning was busy, yet Dawson was never far from my thoughts. If only I knew what the hell to do about him and those kisses.

Chapter Six

DAWSON

"You three are first up in the rotation for training with naloxone," Nick Hudson explained. "I'm starting with y'all because you happen to be the ones who responded to the last overdose. I know it's been weighing on you, but the guy's going to be okay, and that's all that matters."

I leaned back in my chair at the round table where I was seated with Jackson, Wade, and Nick, who was the administrative supervisor for Stolen Hearts Valley Emergency Response. My chest tightened, and cold tension balled in my gut.

Nick was referring to the emergency injections to administer when people accidentally, or not, overdosed on the opiates that were the scourge of society these days. I'd been a first responder for over a decade now. Not much got to me, so I hated how much that one fucking call needled me. I kept seeing that guy's blue face and the pills strewn on the floor beside him. Like a record jumping tracks, my mind immediately skipped back to another night. One I wished I could erase completely from my memory.

"That okay, Dawson?" Nick asked.

"I zoned out. Sorry about that. What time did you say?"

"It's scheduled in two days."

"That'll work."

Jackson interjected. "We can rearrange work around the lodge if anything conflicts with it."

Nick lifted his chin and nodded. "Thanks." Glancing at the clock, he added, "I've got another meeting, so I'll catch you guys at next week's team meeting."

Wade, Jackson, and I stood together and filed out, calling our goodbyes on the way out. Wade had to hurry off, but Jackson leaned against my truck, aiming his way too perceptive gaze on me. "How you doing?"

I took a breath, not getting much air. "Just fine. Why are you asking now?"

"Because you've been cranky as hell the past three weeks. Let me clarify. You haven't been your usual jokester self, which translates to cranky. I know that call got to you. It got to me too."

If only Jackson knew.

Fuck it. Jackson was a good friend, so I might as well tell him. He'd also been through his own share of hell in the military.

"Look, man, I don't talk about my family much, but that was exactly how my dad died. My dad's a fucking asshole, or he *was*. I don't miss him, but that shit scares me." My chest tightened, and I had to pause and take a breath. "He was an asshole, and my mom used to tell me all the time he was self-medicating with his poison of choice at the time. I'm pretty sure I'm not an asshole, but sometimes, things aren't that easy."

Jackson was quiet for several long moments before he bounced his heel against the gravel. "Yeah, that shit scares me too. You're right that you don't talk much about your family. Just enough that I filled in a few blanks on my own. I get it. You know I don't talk much about my own baggage, but I've seen some bad shit go down. You've got the one thing that'll get you through with whatever this is. If you want to talk, I'm here. Even if you don't, I just want you to know I'm here."

I stared at him intently, this time managing to get a decent amount of air in my lungs when I took a breath. "What's that one thing you're talking about?"

"You're aware. That's what matters. Or at least that's what the therapist the military made me see for months told me." Jackson sighed. "Look, she actually helped, so for what it's worth, if you ever—" His words stopped when I shook my head.

"Been there, done that, man. And you're right, some of them help. When I was a kid, we had child protection cycling in and out of our house. My dad drank hardcore. If he'd stuck to that, he'd probably still be alive today. It was the pills that killed him. My mom ... well, she tried, she did, but she couldn't protect us from him. Hell, he beat on her more than us."

Jackson nodded slowly, his gaze steady. That was the thing about Jackson. He didn't push. He was damn perceptive though, and sometimes, that got under my skin. "As I said, I'm here if you need to talk."

"Thanks, man," I said because that was really all I could handle for now.

He pushed away from my truck. "See you back at the lodge."

He was giving me my space, and I knew he knew I needed it.

"Jackson," I called.

The crunch of his boots on the gravel stopped, and he turned to look back at me. "I needed that, so thanks."

Leaning against the bar at Lost Deer, I took a sip of water.

Because the flat truth was I didn't even care to have a beer. Rehashing the call from a few weeks ago had shaken me.

I was losing interest in even escaping. Oddly, I wasn't afraid of the darkness that fell over me occasionally. I'd learned it was something I needed to let wash over me, and I would get through to the other side. I wasn't my father.

Delilah paused in front of me as she set clean glasses in a rack behind the bar. "You doing okay, Dawson?"

"Right as rain, Delilah."

"Not even a beer?"

"Nah. I'm good with this," I replied, lifting my water glass.

"Not even a girl?"

I rolled my eyes. "Not even a girl, Delilah."

I wasn't going to admit I had come out tonight hoping to shake myself loose from this mental fixation on Evie. No such fucking luck.

Don't get me wrong, my body was spun tight and tangled because I was apparently going to become celibate. But no one drew my interest beyond an objective appreciation.

I was in dire straits, especially if Evie continued to shut me out. Intellectually, I understood her hesitation. Hell, I hadn't done a damn thing but play the field since I'd known her. I was fucking determined to shift gears, but I was restless and irritated I couldn't find an outlet in any other way.

Delilah's attention was drawn away by another customer. I slid my empty glass to the edge of the bar and turned to leave. Stepping out into the cool night, I took a breath and leaned my head back to look at the stars. Glimmers of light scattered across the black canvas. The moon hung low over the mountains in the distance.

On the heels of another breath, I looked ahead, striding toward my truck. A short drive later, I was walking the path through the trees behind the lodge. I heard the sound of footsteps and glanced ahead. Evie.

I knew it was Evie primarily by my body's reaction. My

heart kicked against my ribs, and a familiar electricity hummed to life inside.

As if she could sense my eyes on her, she stopped on the path and looked back. Lights along the ground cast a soft glow in the trees. There was just enough illumination for me to see the curve of her hip and the subtle gleam on her dark hair.

She waited until I reached her. My annoyance with losing all interest in anyone else slipped away. The way my body sparked to life the moment I saw her only served to reinforce just how bad I had it for her.

I wished I could understand why this fire had flared up so powerfully. I'd known Evie for two years, and up until a few weeks ago, my interest in her had maybe a bit more kick to it than usual, but it had been nothing like this. It was as if now that a bit of fuel had been added, it was raging out of control.

"Hey, Evie," I drawled, the sound of the leaves rustling under my feet quieting when I came to a stop in front of her.

When her eyes met mine, for a flash, my breath left me. Fuck, she was beautiful. Her dark hair hung around her shoulders, and my eyes fell to her plump lips. When her lopsided smile unfurled, it was like a kick to my libido. Her scent drifted to me, wrapping around me like silken threads. Everything drew tight inside, and my cock throbbed.

Here I was, thinking I could convince her it wasn't just sex I wanted when, sweet Jesus, I wanted her. So badly.

"Hey, Dawson," she replied, her voice low with a rasp to it.

Her voice alone tightened those silken threads, pulling me closer.

I *had* to have her.

I took a breath, keeping my gaze on her. I was speaking before I had cleared my words with my thoughts. "I want you."

Her breath came out in a little surprised puff. Her eyes widened, and a flush crested on her cheeks.

Now that I'd gone and blurted that out, I decided to just go with it. "And I know you want me too."

The moment felt suspended and electric as I waited. I knew I saw the answering flare of desire in her eyes, and I could see the rapid flutter of her pulse in her neck.

I absorbed the sight of her. She wore a skirt that hugged her hips and fell to her ankles in a twirl above a pair of leather cowboy boots. I wondered where she had been.

I hoped like hell she hadn't been on a date. That was certainly something I *never* wondered about any woman. Not in this way. That's how off-kilter she had me. She elicited a combination of raw desire tangled up in an unfamiliar emotion.

"Let's just take it one step at a time," I said, taking an actual step closer and sifting my fingers through her silky hair.

My eyes canted down, noticing her nipples tight against the thin silk of her blouse. I wanted to dip my head and suck on her nipples, right through the silk. I wanted to shove her denim jacket off and strip her.

But that was probably moving too fast.

I stayed quiet and waited. The deep breath she took was audible in the quiet night. After a moment, when I thought the waiting was about to kill me, she nodded. The breath I hadn't even realized I'd been holding came out, hissing through my teeth.

Chapter Seven

EVIE

I could barely hear over the rush of blood pounding through my ears. My pulse had truly gone wild, pounding so hard and fast I was verging on dizzy.

I felt almost hypnotized as I stared into Dawson's eyes. His silvery-gray gaze had darkened, and I recognized the flare of desire.

"Okay," I heard myself saying before I really thought it through.

In all honesty, I couldn't really think, not in Dawson's presence. All he had to do was stand there, and he gave off an aura of sensuality and masculinity that tugged on the fierce arousal in me.

My answer appeared to surprise him. His eyes widened slightly before he stepped closer yet again. I felt as if I were caught in a riptide, and I couldn't swim against the current. It was too strong. All I could do was succumb. Anything else was exhausting and fought against the core of my desire.

I wasn't sure what I expected, but it wasn't for Dawson to move with such deliberation. "Evie," he murmured.

When he brushed my hair away from my face, shivers chased in the wake of his touch. He dusted a kiss on my temple, another beside my ear, and a few along my jawline. With each kiss, his hands sank deeper into my hair until he slid one to cup the nape of my neck. There was the slightest sting on my scalp as his fingers laced into my hair. The subtle pain felt good. I was buffeted by need, and being able to anchor myself to a concrete sensation was almost a relief.

His lips hadn't even met mine yet, and I was utterly undone. Everything was slow. I felt like hot lava inside and could hardly catch my breath.

"Dawson," I gasped when he pressed a kiss to the corner of my mouth.

"Yes?"

His lips were but a whisper from mine when he spoke, and I could feel the subtle motion of them brushing over mine. He still didn't kiss me.

"Are you sure?"

Instead of answering, I leaned forward, angling up just enough to catch his lips with mine. His low growl escaped into our kiss right before it went wild. We were on kiss three now, and maybe the third time was the charm. The moment his tongue slid across the seam of my lips and mine opened on a sigh, it felt as if we were caught in a roaring current of need and desire, and absolutely nothing could stop it.

Dawson stepped closer until he was flush against me, and I could feel the hard ridge of his arousal. Deepening our kiss, he angled my head to the side, and his tongue stroked against mine.

Liquid fire spun through my veins. I was so hot I could hardly stand as my body quivered with desire. He worked my mouth and then drew back, dusting slow, sweet kisses on the corners before diving in again. By the time he lifted his head, I was gasping, nearly ready to beg him to fuck me, right here and right now.

His voice punctured the haze of need filling my mind.

"What?" I managed to ask, my lips feeling so puffy and swollen from our kiss that my words came out slurred.

"I said someone's coming. Your place or mine?"

He didn't step back, and I didn't want him to. I was so far gone I couldn't quite make myself care that someone might see us like this. It could be any number of people we worked with or guests walking to their cabin, but I simply didn't care. Not even a little.

My mind managed to latch onto the one thing that seemed to matter at this moment—which place was closest—so I said, "Yours."

He stepped back, instantly leaving me bereft. I loved the feel of his heat and strength encompassing me, and I didn't want to lose it. He caught my hand in his and turned, walking swiftly through the trees as he angled off the main path.

Within a few minutes, we reached his cabin, tucked in the trees just like the others. My heart was still pounding like mad, and my legs felt like rubber, but curiosity kicked in when he opened the door. He held the door for me, waiting until I had stepped inside before following me and closing it.

Just like all the cabins, the sensor activated the lights when we stepped inside. The two lamps in the corners cast a soft glow in the space. His cabin was mine in reverse. There was a four-poster bed with pillows piled high and a fluffy down quilt, a dresser to the side, and a bench against the wall with hooks above it by the door. The small kitchen tucked in one corner had a narrow counter that held a microwave, a small sink, a tiny refrigerator, and a coffeemaker.

Beyond that was the door I knew led to a luxurious bathroom with a large tub and shower. Jackson had spared no expense for the guest cabins and was gracious enough to let staff stay in them as a major side benefit to working here.

Although there were no personal decorations, the space still felt like Dawson somehow. One of his worn denim jackets was hanging by the door, and several pairs of his battered work boots were on the floor beneath.

I was suddenly unsure, but I wasn't about to stop. Before I could think too much, which was a good thing, I felt the heat of Dawson's palm land between my shoulder blades and slide down. I was turning into him as he angled toward me. Our kiss picked up right where we left off.

It started slow but quickly picked up in speed and intensity. He was devouring my mouth while I couldn't get close enough fast enough. I was on my tippy toes, one hand mapping the surface of his chest and the other wrapped around his waist, clinging to the corded muscles along his spine. I couldn't help it, I had to feel his ass after admiring it from afar for two damn years.

Dawson Marsh had one fine ass—hard and muscled just like the rest of him. I slid my hand down over the denim, savoring the flex of his muscles under my touch.

His lips broke free from mine. I heard the amusement in his voice when he said, "I guess I don't have to worry about you accusing me of copping a feel."

I bit my lip and shook my head. "Not at all."

Somehow, this light moment only amped up the intensity between us. I didn't know what to make of any of this. All I knew was I wanted Dawson, and I didn't care to contemplate all the reasons it was a potentially disastrous idea.

I couldn't have said if it was truly that my need for Dawson was that profound, or if my somewhat limited experience with men made it hard for me to contend with the sheer force of the raw desire burning hot and high between us. High school had been one long dry spell for me. After I got past it, I'd had a few boyfriends, but no one who blew me away. Grace was right, though. I'd been complaining about how little sex I'd had of late.

I supposed it was because I was hoping for a little something more than yet another foray into the dating scene, which was usually way too casual for me. Yet here I was, diving into the madness with a man who specialized in friends with benefits. Even though a tiny voice in a closet in the back of my mind tried to tell me I shouldn't expect anything from Dawson, I couldn't bring myself to listen.

The need rushing through me was a riptide, and I was well out to sea already.

Restless for more, I stepped back slightly, kicking off my boots and shrugging out of my jacket. I moved to unbutton my blouse, pausing when Dawson's hand caught one of my wrists. His touch was light, yet it might as well have been a brand. Fire flashed over my skin under his fingers, radiating up my arm.

When I looked up, he shook his head. "Not yet. I don't want to rush this."

The sensual promise contained in his words sent a blast of heat through me. I swallowed and nodded, watching as he toed his shoes off and kicked them to the side. He hadn't worn a jacket. I caught the hem of his T-shirt and slid it up, my breath coming out in a gasp at the feel of his warm skin.

Catching his eyes, I said, "We don't have to rush, but I want this off."

He ran his tongue over his teeth as his mouth kicked up at one corner. The flare of heat in his eyes nearly buckled my knees. I meant what I said. I'd seen Dawson shirtless from a distance, but I wanted the view up close and personal. Now.

He obliged, reaching behind his head and pulling his shirt up and over in one swoop. Sweet Jesus. My mouth went dry, and there was a pull low in my belly. His skin was burnished gold and lightly dusted with hair. His chest was cut muscle with his abs delineated clearly.

I meant to say something, but it was lost when he stepped closer, nudging me back until my knees hit the edge of the mattress. His hands slid down my sides as he kissed me. His palms curled around my hips and lifted me onto the mattress. I felt the hard ridge of his arousal briefly before he stretched me out on the bed. I couldn't help but savor how easily he manhandled me.

The mattress dipped under his weight as he lay beside me, his palm coming to rest on my belly, branding me with its heat. My breath came shallow and fast. I was almost shaking with need—hot and shivery all over.

Glancing up, I found Dawson's eyes waiting for me—dark and smoky, a stormy sky waiting to be unleashed. Simply looking at him set my heart to kicking even faster.

Restless, I shifted my legs. It was hard to bear the intensity of his gaze. I was almost relieved when his hand slid up to cup one of my breasts. A ragged gasp escaped when he brushed his thumb over my taut, achy nipple. Dipping his head, his mouth closed over the other, right through my blouse and bra. The friction combined with the suction sent a jolt of pleasure straight to my sex.

When I arched into him, I felt the moisture between my thighs, my panties wet as slick heat built in my channel. He teased my nipples until I was gasping and pleading with him. Only then, only when I actually said please did he flick the buttons loose on my blouse, the cool air hitting my skin as I sighed in relief.

"Dawson, please ..." I gasped.

I didn't beg. *Ever*. Until now. Of all the men whose name I thought I would be crying out, Dawson's wasn't it. I was so caught up in the power of the desire rushing between us that I didn't care. I had absolutely no shame whatsoever.

So much of this was startling. Perhaps the most shocking of all was the depth of comfort I felt. A strange sense of freedom lay within the ease in the desire blooming between us. I had no doubt he experienced the same force I did.

He lifted his head, his thumb resting over the clasp between my breasts. "Please what?"

My eyelids were heavy. I felt almost drugged, intoxicated with the potency of his presence and his strength surrounding me. I managed to drag my eyes open to find his silver smoky gaze waiting for me. I didn't even know what I was begging for. I just knew I needed release.

I shifted my hips where his knee had settled between my thighs, the weight of it tightening the fabric of my skirt. The subtle restraint spun into the need driving me. I wanted to be bare naked with him deep inside me. As soon as possible, preferably.

"I need this off," I said, wiggling my shoulders.

He had me pinned in such a way that I couldn't move very well. However, it didn't feel controlling, and sweet hell, I did *not* want him to move. Rather, I wanted some sort of magic trick where my clothes simply flew off.

"Soon," he replied.

I rocked my hips, pressing against the hot ridge of his cock. Satisfaction rushed through me when he closed his eyes, and a low growl escaped. I loved knowing he might be close to losing control.

Then his mouth was on mine again, and I lost myself in a hot, wet kiss. Blessedly, he flicked my bra open and tossed it aside, and I could finally feel his bare skin against mine. The light dusting of hair on his chest abraded my nipples, and I gasped into his mouth.

I kept trying to rush Dawson, but he refused. Again and again, he drove me to the brink of madness. By the time his lips were mapping their way across my belly, my breath was coming in sharp pants.

Finally, *finally*, he rose, his palms gliding down my sides to catch the waistband of my skirt. Happy to help, I lifted my hips as he slid it down over my legs, and I kicked it free from my ankles. Frantic for more, I hooked a finger in the edge of my panties only to feel his hand curl over mine and hear his low command. "Not yet."

"Oh, my God!" I burst out. "You're bossy."

His answering chuckle sent shivers chasing over my skin as he leaned down and trailed hot kisses up the inside of my thigh. He released my hand, his palm sliding in a heated path over the sensitive skin along the inside of my hip. With gentle pressure, he nudged my thighs apart.

I was quivering, wondering distantly if I could climax without him ever touching me where I so desperately wanted his touch. My hips bucked when his fingers trailed over the wet silk. His stubble grazed across the skin on my thigh, the slight sensation spinning into and heightening all the others racing through me. I felt as if I were going to fly apart.

He muttered something before rising and doing me the favor of finally sliding my panties down over my legs. My thighs were damp from my arousal.

"Evie, you're soaked, sweetheart. Prettiest pussy I ever saw."

My belly flipped at his blunt appraisal and the way he said *sweetheart*. My orgasm almost crashed over me when he teased his fingers through my slick heat. I bit my lip to keep from moaning.

He seemed to sense just how close to the edge I was. When my hips rocked into his touch, he sank two thick fingers into my core and circled his thumb over my clit. In seconds, I was crying out, chanting his name and telling him I couldn't wait anymore.

His fingers delved deeper, and he swirled his tongue around my clit. Pleasure exploded, narrowing to the sharp point at my center and scattering hot sparks through my body as I shuddered. My orgasm hit me so hard, I was nearly incoherent when he drew back.

I lay there, gasping for air with aftershocks of pleasure ricocheting through me. This was all too much. I usually had it together enough to be able to return the favor, but I could say I'd never been with anyone like this. It was too hot; a burgeoning desire that fed into itself and gained power with each step along the way.

When I felt Dawson move away, I managed to open my eyes to see him standing and kicking his jeans free. He caught them in one hand, tugging his wallet out and tossing a condom on the bed beside me.

When his briefs followed, my mouth watered to see all of him bared to me. Dawson was a glorious specimen of a man. His body was tall and rangy, his easy strength evident in the grace of every movement.

Despite the pleasure still pinging through my body, need began to build inside me again. I reached for him. I felt caught, held fast in the grip of a desire so pure, I didn't think it would be slaked until he was buried inside me.

Even then, I didn't know if that would be enough.

"Hurry," I heard myself say, my voice ragged.

Snatching the condom off the bed, he ripped the packet with his teeth. His smoky gaze held mine as he rolled it on, the mattress dipping with his weight when his knee landed between my thighs. In a flash, his hard, muscled body came down over me. I sighed, curling my legs around his hips, frantic for him to fill me.

The thick crown of his cock nudged at my entrance. His hands slid up my sides, catching mine in his and stretching my arms over my head. I felt exposed.

"Last chance," he murmured.

His hips rocked slightly into mine, the slide of his thick cock over my swollen clit sending a sharp, piercing pleasure through me.

On the heels of that, I gasped, "Last chance for what?"

"To tell me you don't want this to go any further."

My heart squeezed hard inside my chest. Not that there was any question about what I wanted at this point. Yet, somehow, for him to be explicit about it right in the heat of this, to insist I make it clear what I wanted, made me feel so cared for I was awash in emotion. I couldn't focus on that now. I needed this—this thrumming, out of control desire—to let me shy away from just what it all might mean.

There was absolutely no doubt.

"Don't you dare stop now," I panted when he rocked into me once again, teasing my entrance with his cock.

Chapter Eight

DAWSON

Evie's dark hair was in a tangle against the white pillows, her lips plump and puffy from our kisses, and her skin glistening as she looked at me. No matter how desperately I wanted her, I meant what I said. If she called it off now, I would stop.

Thank fuck she didn't change her mind, though, because I wanted this more than I'd *ever* wanted anything. I didn't know what this was between us, but it was something I'd never felt before.

I loved women, I loved sex, and I loved having fun.

Yet *this*? This thing with Evie was beyond my control and well beyond the horizons of my experience. The only thing keeping me leashed to reality was the pleasure I gave her.

The kind of discipline I needed with her was different. Usually, I enjoyed the chase, but I never lost control of the moment. With every breath she took, with every soft sound that came from the back of her throat, and with every move she made, I was in danger of losing all control.

I honestly wasn't sure I wouldn't come the second I sank inside her. Her juices were slick against me, the core of her calling to me. I could feel the damp peaks of her nipples pressing against my chest, the rapid rise and fall of her chest from her breath, and her heart beating against mine. I dipped my head, catching her lips in a messy, wet kiss.

Lifting my head to gulp in some air, I clenched her hands in mine, lacing our fingers together. I adjusted the angle of my hips, notching the head of my cock at the sweet heat of her core.

On a breath, I sank into her slowly, sheathing myself inside her rippling, slick channel. As I expected, release threatened the moment I was deep inside her. I held still, gritting my teeth because I didn't want this to end. Not just yet.

Evie sighed, arching her hips into me. I drew back again and then again, sinking inside, each stroke into her a decadent pleasure. She made these little soft whimpers, and the sound nearly drove me crazy. I released one of her hands, needing her to find her release before my own overtook me.

Reaching between us, I teased through her curls and pressed on her clit. As her eyes fell closed, she cried out, her channel clamping down around my cock. Only then did I let go. With one more stroke, my climax raced through me. Everything went taut, the release slamming through me so hard I couldn't hold myself up.

Her arms came around me when I fell against her. I rolled us over, holding her tight as my cock stayed buried inside her. I wasn't letting go. Not now. Maybe not ever.

This would usually be the time when I would somehow tease and tactfully disengage. Yet I didn't with her. I couldn't move, and I didn't want to move. I felt the soft gust of her breath on my shoulder, acutely aware of her warm, damp skin on mine.

I held her close as my heartbeat slowed, and I sifted my fingers through her hair. When she started to stir, I said, "Stay."

Sometime during the night, I woke. Evie was curled up beside me, her sweet bottom pressing into my arousal.

I had a rule. I didn't sleep with women, but I hadn't even hesitated to break it last night. It would be easy to chalk it up to sex, but all I cared about at this moment was Evie, soft and warm in my arms. I slept better last night than I'd slept in years even though it had only been a few hours. Opening my eyes, I glanced at the clock on the nightstand. It read 2:30 a.m.

I told myself to ignore the ache of my cock, but then Evie had to go and shift her hips slightly. Being so fucking turned on, I could've come right then.

I breathed through it, trying to talk my body down, yet I couldn't. All my effort was to no avail. She sighed. I felt when she came awake, a subtle hum of energy coursing through her body.

"Dawson?" Her voice was soft in the dark, husky with sleep.

I slid my hand up her side from where it was resting on the curve of her hip. "Yes?" I murmured into her hair.

"Oh." A raspy laugh followed.

Evie snuggled closer again, and my good intentions were hard to cling to. Especially when she reached her hand between us, shifting just enough to slide her palm over the length of my cock. I gave in.

It was a slow, sleepy encounter—so sensual and so hot, it left me slayed. She was hot and slick when I nudged into her from behind. We fucked in the darkness with nothing more than the subtle motion of our hips rocking together. It was only when she began to ripple around me that my own release followed, pouring into her. Abruptly, I realized what I'd forgotten.

The moment was almost ruined. I tensed. "Fuck, I'm sorry, Evie. I forgot a condom," I said, feeling like an idiot and trying to gather myself from the emotional disarray inside.

My palm was resting on her belly, and she slid her hand over it, lacing her fingers through mine. “I just remembered too. If you’re worried, I’m on the pill. I suppose I should freak out, but for some reason, I trust you’re clean. I know I am. It’s been almost two years since I’ve even been with anyone.”

If I hadn’t already been jolted wide-awake by my recognition of what had just happened, that little nugget of information had my eyes flying wide open in the darkness. With a mental shake, I focused on what she said. “I promise I’m clean. I don’t even remember the last time I had sex without a condom.”

I relaxed against her when I felt her nod although my mind was spinning. I didn’t know what to make of the fact that I was so far gone over her I’d forgotten a condom. There was that and her stunning admission that it had been two years since she’d been with anyone.

She squeezed my hand. “Okay,” she said, her voice still sleepy.

Not more than a minute or two passed before I felt her breathing shift into sleep. For a few minutes, I thought I would have trouble falling back to sleep. The ramifications of just how thoroughly my guard had dropped with her had me internally stumbling in a rush of panic, but I let it go. I couldn’t quite help it, not buried inside her while she fell asleep. Sleep claimed me as well.

When I woke hours later, Evie was gone, and the sheets were cool on that side of the bed. I missed her instantly.

Chapter Nine

EVIE

“More coffee?” I asked, pausing beside the table of a family.

When the woman nodded, I filled her coffee and moved to check on the next table. It was Saturday morning and busy. With guests at the lodge, there were always customers for breakfast, but on the weekends, we usually fielded a rush of locals on top of that. Dani’s weekend brunch menu was legendary in Stolen Hearts Valley and the surrounding towns.

Glancing over my shoulder, I saw the waiting area was still full. I took a breath, jotted down the next order, and hurried off to the kitchen. Despite how busy I was, Dawson crowded my thoughts. I’d replayed far too many heated moments from last night in my mind.

When I woke up this morning with a start, I’d all but run out of there. I was never one who needed an alarm clock. I generally woke on my own, usually a few minutes before any alarm clock I had went off, yet I had almost overslept today. I’d been relieved at the need to rush out of his place. If Dawson had woken, I had an excuse for why I had to leave without saying goodbye.

Fortunately, my shift started at 5:30 a.m. Dawn was barely there, and I'd been able to do my imaginary walk of shame with nothing but a glimmer of the sun on the horizon.

My body quaked with a memory, suddenly recalling the feel of him over me as he filled me; the stretch so delicious, so decadent I could still feel the echoes of its pleasure.

"Watch it, Evie," Grace said, her voice startling me.

I skidded to a stop after I pushed through the swinging door into the kitchen. Grace was balancing a massive tray carefully on her shoulder.

"Sorry! I didn't see you." I set down my empty tray on the table right beside the door. "Want some help?"

At her nod, I followed her back out into the restaurant, snagging one of the tray stands and setting it out for her when she reached the table. We all did this kind of thing for each other when we had a moment.

"Who's got the waffles?" I asked, lifting a plate piled high with waffles topped with fresh strawberries and whipped cream.

"Omelet with tomatoes, spinach, and cream cheese?" Grace called.

We had the table served and happy within minutes. As we walked back, Grace asked in a low voice, "What's with you this morning?"

Glancing at her as we stepped back into the kitchen, I shrugged. "Sorry, just a little tired." Now definitely wasn't the time to talk, so I was relieved when one of the line cooks called up one of my orders. "Gotta get this," I murmured.

The morning spun by in a blur of orders being called out, endless coffees filled, and empty plates stacked by the dishwasher. The morning madness finally slowed, and I finished my shift, having taken the early breakfast one. I untied my apron as I stepped into the staff kitchen. The door swung shut behind me, muffling the hum of the restaurant. I paused to lean against the wall as I tossed my apron into a laundry bin by the door.

I had managed a few breaths when I felt Dawson's presence before I even saw him. Looking up, my heart instantly started to pound. He stood by the counter that ran alongside the wall as he filled a mug with coffee.

He turned, his gaze lasering to mine almost instantly. With my pulse galloping off, one look in his eyes caused my breath to catch in my throat. He slowly lifted the cup of coffee, taking a sip and never once looking away.

After he lowered his mug, he drawled, "Mornin', Evie."

I managed a shallow breath and swallowed. "Good morning," I croaked.

I couldn't seem to move and just stood there staring at him. My breath came light and fast while my heart beat in tune to the rapid sound of a knife chopping in the kitchen behind me.

Gesturing over my shoulder, I said, "I had the early shift."

Why, oh why, I felt the need to point that out, I didn't know.

"I gathered," Dawson replied, a teasing glint entering his eyes.

I felt funny. My heart was practically running a race, my skin was tingling all over, and my belly was fluttering. This was no big deal. I needed to get some kind of a grip.

Just then, the door to the back of the kitchen pushed open, and Dani hurried through, her arms filled with a stack of dish towels and napkins. "Mornin', Dawson," she called over her shoulder as she blew past him.

"Let me help," I said, pushing away from the wall and hurrying after her.

Not that I minded work, and I would've offered to help regardless, but I was blessedly relieved to have some sort of excuse to run away from Dawson.

"Aren't you done with your shift?" Dani asked when I turned with her as she pushed through the door into the main kitchen.

The usual cacophony of the line cooks talking and the activity of people bustling in and out from the front hit me. "Oh yeah, I'm just finishing up, but I'll help you with this."

Dani didn't argue the point with me. As soon as we reached the front, I took the stack from her and put the towels and napkins away on the shelves above the prep station. After that, I had no excuse to linger. Unfortunately, no one was sick or had called out, so I couldn't offer to help cover the next shift either. I was torn between wishing Dawson was still in the back and hoping he was gone.

I didn't even realize I was holding my breath until I pushed through the door to find him still there but talking with Dani.

"Hey, Evie," Dani called. "Mind going with Dawson for a run to the supply store in Asheville?"

Fuck, fuck, fuck.

I could feel the heat of Dawson's gaze on me and refused to look at him. This was all a mess.

"I'm leaving in a half hour, going to pick up some stuff at the building supply place," he began. "It sounds like Dani needs some things from the kitchen distributor. Happy for you to ride along."

"Please, Evie," Dani implored. "I'm going to meet with Valentina to go over some accounting stuff, and I have a doctor's appointment this afternoon."

I couldn't say no. I would look like a bitch, and I had no good reason to say no.

"Sure," I replied, striving to keep my tone casual. There was no reason for me to feel nervous. There was no reason for this to be a loaded question. But now that I said yes, that meant several hours alone with Dawson.

My heart practically did cartwheels. When I finally let myself look at Dawson, I saw his lips quirk slightly at the corners. Normally, he would tease me far more bluntly right about now, and I would throw it right back at him, but I was too unsettled after last night. I could *not* believe what I had allowed to happen.

Twice.

Chapter Ten

EVIE

I had never been so aware of the size of a truck cab in my life. I'd honestly never even thought about it, but the space between Dawson and me felt taut, crowded with all that had passed between us the night before.

This was not the first time I had done errands for the lodge with him, yet this time was different. More than once, I caught my gaze sliding sideways to look at him and then yanked it forward again. Today was one of those perfect days in the Blue Ridge Mountains, and the view was quite beautiful. With autumn taking hold, the trees were a kaleidoscope of red, gold, orange, and purple. The mountains' namesake blue haze shimmered above. The day was beautiful, bordering on magical.

We were about halfway into the hour and a half drive to Asheville when I did the math and realized that with the errands Dani had assigned to us, we would be together for almost eight hours. Eight hours alone with Dawson was a special form of torture.

A mingled sense of anticipation and anxiety coiled in my

chest. I was rattled. The intimacy of last night echoed inside.

I pointlessly brushed my hands over my thighs, the denim smooth under my palms. He hadn't even turned on the radio, and I felt too childish to ask.

As if clued in to my restlessness, Dawson asked, "How ya doing over there, Evie?"

"Fine. I'm fine."

He was quiet for a beat, and I dared to glance in his direction. With the angle of the sun, his profile was cast in shadow. His cheekbones were almost pretty, sculpted with a clean line. His nose was slightly large with a tiny hitch on one side. He had full, generous lips, and just thinking about how they felt on mine last night made my skin hot and prickly.

His eyes slid sideways, snagging mine. I was so accustomed to his teasing manner that the flicker of uncertainty in his gaze startled me. He looked as if he didn't know what to do with me like this.

I could understand the feeling. I felt as if a mini earthquake had occurred in my body, one quite specific to him. I wasn't sure what to do with myself.

Giving in to the desire flashing hot and high between us last night had been impulsive, and part of me regretted it. I felt the heat blooming on my neck and cheeks.

He looked away, and I breathed a tiny sigh of relief. Just as I was trying to figure out what to say, he spoke. "So is this how it's going to be?"

"What do you mean?"

"Are we going to pretend last night never happened?"

My heart tumbled, and I had to take a steadying breath. "I'm not ..." Pausing, I gave my head a little shake. "I'm not trying to pretend last night didn't happen. I just ..."

God, I hated this. I was all a muddle inside and felt so foolish. Twisting my hands together, I tried again. "I didn't expect last night, and now I don't know what to think."

Dawson's eyes stayed on the road as he replied, "Well, that's two of us then."

The tension that was bundled inside me eased slowly. Somehow, it helped to know I wasn't alone in this.

"What do you want?" I blurted out.

My question surprised me. I wasn't surprised at the question itself because it had been tumbling through my mind ever since our first kiss. Rather, I was surprised I wanted to know so badly that my words got ahead of my thoughts. I hadn't given myself time to consider the ramifications.

He took an exit off the highway, slowing onto a side road that would lead us to downtown Asheville. When he came to a stop at the light, he looked over, his gaze somber.

Although I'd known Dawson for two years, I didn't *know* him beyond a superficial level—mostly as a teasing playboy who was uniquely skilled at getting under my skin sometimes. Another facet I knew was that he was a good guy. He was always quick to offer to help with anything and generous with his humor. From what I knew from the guys he worked with, he was a hard worker and dedicated.

Last night had overturned all my assumptions about Dawson. While desire had always been an undercurrent between us, I had ignored it and chalked it up as mostly one-sided on my part and nothing more than typical for Dawson since he flirted with abandon.

When he came to a stop at an intersection, his gaze swung to me, intent and searching. I felt compelled to say something.

"Look, I said it when we talked before, but I'm not ..."

Jesus, I couldn't seem to finish a sentence. I stopped when he shook his head.

"Are you gonna tell me again you're not my type?"

I meant to say yes and argue the point, but I didn't. Instead, I shook my head wildly, my face hot. Something about him stripped the niceties away, and I couldn't keep a polite façade in place.

He leaned forward, slipping a hand around the nape of my neck, his lips colliding with mine. His kiss was hard and fierce, his tongue sweeping in to slick against mine. He ended it just as swiftly, pulling away as he gentled, then catching my bottom lip with his teeth and letting it go with a little pop.

A horn honked behind us. He tore his eyes away, looking forward and driving through the intersection. My heart was kicking against my ribs, sensation spinning through me as I tried to catch my breath.

"If that doesn't tell you whether you're my type, I don't know what else will," he said flatly, the bare confidence in his words widening the cracks in the walls around my heart.

I wanted to protest, but I couldn't bring myself to do it. I might not know what to do with any of it, but I knew last night was something different.

As much as I wanted to chalk it up to the beyond amazing sex we had, that wasn't it. It wasn't Dawson's oh, so skilled touch that had me rattled. I had no doubt he'd have brought me to climax without that searing intimacy catching us in a shimmering web. If sex was music, last night had been a song with the magic of an unexpected moment all coming together and setting a stage on fire.

When he came to another intersection, he looked over again. "I guess I thought you were gonna argue with me," he offered with a low laugh.

I twisted my fingers together again, spinning a ring that belonged to my sister on my pinky. "No," I finally said, my voice just above a whisper while my heartbeat thundered through my body.

He nodded, this time looking forward just as the light turned green. "I meant what I said last night."

"What was that again?"

I honestly didn't know what he was referring to. We had said quite a few things to each other, but much of it had been begging, pleading, dirty words, and his name. I was instantly hot, recalling when he called my name with a rough shout as he found his release.

"When I told you we would take it one step at a time," he explained.

Oh. *Oh*.

I felt so dizzy and thrown off balance because I didn't know how to handle this side of Dawson.

"I keep expecting you to crack a joke," I offered.

His smile flashed as quickly as it faded when he glanced over. "I joke a lot but not all the time. Not right now."

I couldn't believe what I asked next. "So by one step at a time, does that involve you trolling the bars for your usual hookups?"

This time, his eyes narrowed when he looked my way. "Fuck no, Evie. I don't hook up as much as you think I do anyway. I won't deny I'm a hell of a flirt, but it's not always something I see through." I could've sworn I saw pain flicker in the depths of his smoky gaze. "I get why you said it, but that's not how I think of you."

Okay, now, I didn't know what the hell to think.

The ring was warm under my fingers as I twisted it. "I guess I made some assumptions. Seeing as I hate when people do that to me, I'm sorry."

Dawson's shoulder lifted in an easy shrug. "It's okay. We all do sometimes. I can't say I haven't done plenty to create that impression."

I hadn't realized we had approached the outskirts of Asheville. Dawson stopped at another intersection and glanced my way. "Your call, where do you want to go first?"

"Let's take care of the building supplies. It'll be quieter at the restaurant supply store later this afternoon."

A short drive later, I followed Dawson around the massive warehouse for building supplies. He was all business, a side of him I'd rarely seen. He stocked up on lumber, all kinds of hardware, and even haggled down the price for some mismatched lumber. By the time we were done almost two hours later, I was starving.

I didn't intend to say anything about it, but my stomach gave me away with a hearty growl once we climbed back into his truck. I slapped my hand over my belly, and Dawson chuckled.

"I was just about to ask if you wanted to grab lunch. I'll take that as a yes."

My stomach, disobeying the hand trying to keep it quiet, let another growl loose. "I'm starving," I offered with a sheepish smile.

"I gathered," he said dryly. "Any requests?"

"Not really. Why don't you pick?"

"In that case, we're going to my favorite diner," he replied as he turned the steering wheel.

Quiet filled the space while my body was anything but—zinging and humming with this inconvenient desire for Dawson. It had been easier to be around him when I had something to pay attention to, even if it was just lumber. My eyes landed on his hand resting over the steering wheel.

He had good hands—strong and slightly battered with a few scars and a light dusting of blond hair. His fingers were long and thick. Unfortunately for me, I knew just how *good* they felt buried inside me. He was, um, *quite* good with his hands. I recalled the calloused surface of his palm coasting over my skin. The memory was visceral and sent my belly into a spinning flip.

Chapter Eleven

EVIE

Dawson pulled up in front of a tiny restaurant tucked between what appeared to be two office buildings. It was a rather nondescript square building with a bright pink sign that read *Candy's Diner*.

Bemused, I followed him inside. He held the door for me, his hand sliding down my back as we stepped through. With a coaxing pressure, he angled me toward the corner. Seconds after we slid into a booth, an older woman arrived at the table wearing large pink glasses with her gray hair tied into a bun held in place by a pen stuck through it.

She smiled brightly, pulling a notepad out of her black apron tied over a pair of jeans and a white T-shirt. "Well, hey there, Dawson Marsh. You finally brought a date for lunch."

Dawson's return smile was wide. "Hey, Candy, this is my friend Evie," he said, gesturing toward me.

Candy's smile immediately lifted my spirits. The warmth and ease she gave off was comforting. "Nice to meet you, Evie. I'm Candy, and welcome to my diner. What can I get you two?"

"I'll take a coffee to start. You?" he asked, his eyes

swinging to mine.

"Definitely some coffee. Let me look at the menu," I replied, pulling one of the menus out from where they were tucked between the condiments in the center of the table.

"I'll be right back with those coffees. Everything is served all day, so get whatever you want, hon," Candy said before turning away.

Opening my menu, I paused to look around. The diner was small with booths along the walls and tables scattered in the center. A counter along the back offered a view of part of the kitchen. The décor was simple. The booths and tables were polished wood with silverware rolled up in paper napkins in front of each seat. Photographs lined the wall behind the counter, and bright pink curtains hung in the windows.

Glancing at Dawson, I smiled. "Candy seems nice."

"Oh, she's nice all right, the best kind of person. She's salt of the earth. I knew her before I moved here. In fact, she's the one who told me about the job at the lodge."

"How do you know her?" I asked.

He had glanced down to open his menu, so I followed suit, perusing the options as he answered. "Candy and her husband used to live where I grew up near the coast. She grew up in the mountains, and they decided to move back and take over this diner when her mom got sick. They're good people. I'll take you back in the kitchen and introduce you to her husband before we go."

Although Dawson clearly felt affection toward Candy and her husband, there was a subdued quality when he spoke of where he grew up. I wanted to know why.

Candy arrived with our coffees, and I followed Dawson's lead to order what he described as the "best biscuits and gravy in the universe."

After Candy departed for the kitchen again, I said, "So tell me about where you grew up. Is your family still there?"

Dawson—usually so easygoing and quick to joke—had a

blank look on his face for a beat before his eyes shuttered. Although I knew next to nothing about his family or his hometown, I knew instantly his childhood didn't contain happy memories.

He took a sip of his coffee, tracing his thumb over the curve of the mug handle after he set it down before he spoke. "I grew up a stone's throw from the coast. If you've been to the North Carolina coast ..." At my nod, he cracked a smile, and continued, "You know it's busy. Anyway, we didn't have much. It was just me, my mom, my dad, and my younger brother. We were poor, and I surfed. I stay in touch with my mom and my brother, but my dad passed away about six years ago."

Dawson's words were calm, level to the point that it was as if he had recited them many times. I had *so* many questions, yet I sensed now wasn't the time for them.

"I'm sorry about your father," I said softly.

He nodded tightly and took another swallow of his coffee. Undercurrents rippled, yet with his eyes flat and his lips tightening, it was clear the topic of his father wasn't a good one.

"What does your brother do?" I asked, figuring perhaps that was a safer topic.

"He took over my father's construction business after my dad passed away. We're not too close, but we stay in touch."

"And your mom?" I asked, wondering why I pressed ahead. My curiosity was getting the better of me. There was more to Dawson than the surface he showed to the world, and I was curious, always so curious.

"My mom does the books for that same business, always has. She's got some health problems now, but she still handles that."

Something flickered in his gaze, and my heart gave a little squeeze.

"What about you?" he asked, shifting the topic away from himself.

For a moment, my curiosity pressed again, but when I looked into his silver-smoke eyes, I wanted the pain lingering there to dissipate. "You already know I grew up right around Stolen Hearts Valley. You'll meet my older brother, Mack, sometime because he's planning to move back home. I'm close to my parents, but they were kind of strict. Things were really hard after my sister died." I paused and shrugged, feeling the same thing I usually felt when I thought about my parents—just "not enough." After Krista died, the aftershocks of that event continued to ripple in all our lives.

"I get the parent stuff. You can love someone, and it doesn't mean they're perfect," Dawson said with a slightly bitter smile.

Staring over at him, it felt as if so much more was contained within his words, yet all I could do was nod. Candy's arrival with the promised biscuits and gravy was timely.

"Here you two go. Now, you tell me if they're not delicious, hon," she said with a wink.

"Red's food won't let me down," Dawson drawled.

Candy reached out and squeezed his shoulder, her touch motherly. "Red would never let you down, hon."

When Dawson smiled, the shadows that had entered his gaze when we were talking about his family disappeared. Candy spun away, and he tucked into his food. I took a bite and actually moaned out loud. The light and fluffy biscuits were that kind of absolutely perfect Southern biscuit—buttery, flaky, and just this side of heaven. The gravy was melt-in-your-mouth to die for.

"Oh, my God," I said when I finished chewing, "these are heaven. How come you didn't bring me here before?"

Dawson chuckled and shrugged. His gaze was warm on me, and I wanted to reach across the table and squeeze his hand. My heart did a little funny tumble in my chest, and I took another bite. I wanted another bite, but more than that, I needed something to distract me.

The meal was beyond delicious. I was quite full by the time I finished and shoved my plate to the end of the table. "I'm going to be useless for shopping after this."

Dawson winked. "Good thing we got the lumber taken care of this morning."

"Oh, don't go thinking you're done with the heavy stuff. You know what the kitchen orders are like—boxes and boxes and more boxes."

"Give me half an hour, and I'll be fine. I'm gonna run to the restroom. Be right back."

He stood, tugging his jeans up slightly as he turned away from the table. I didn't mind taking a nice long look at his ass. I couldn't help but stare. With his sun-kissed hair, silver-smoke eyes, and that rangy, lean body of his that I was now intimately acquainted with, well, I sighed a little just thinking about it.

I hadn't noticed Candy at the table right beside us. "He sure is easy on the eyes, isn't he?" she asked, pausing beside our booth.

My cheeks had to be fire engine red by the time I looked up at her. Although I knew she wasn't technically his mother, she sure felt like it.

She laughed softly, giving my shoulder a light squeeze. "Oh, hon, don't worry about it. I imagine most girls look their fill." She gathered our empty plates, stacking them on a tray she set on the table. "You're the first girl he's ever brought here, you know?"

My pulse leaped at that news, and I took a sip of coffee to buy myself a minute. "I didn't know that," I finally said.

"I didn't think you did."

Candy's gaze was assessing. I felt as if I were being weighed and measured to determine if I met whatever imaginary standards she'd set for Dawson, a man she clearly cared about.

She cocked her head to the side as if she had made a decision. "Dawson's a good man, and he brought you here, so you mean something to him. Don't be fooled by his joking. Oh, he's a flirt, all right, probably the worst sort. But I always figured if he really liked a girl, he would be all in. He's that kind of man."

Conveniently or not, someone at a booth on the other side of the restaurant called Candy's name. With a last look, she added, "You seem like a nice girl. Just don't break his heart. Trust me, he's already had it broken, though maybe not in the way you think." With that, she started to turn away, glancing back at the last moment. "It was very nice to meet you, Evie."

My manners got me through the moment even though her comment rattled me. "You as well. The meal was delicious. Thank you."

Dawson returned a few moments later, unknowingly giving me just enough time to gather myself. I knew without a doubt Dawson had spent plenty of time in Asheville. The guys from the lodge sometimes came here together for some fun beyond the boundaries of Stolen Hearts Valley.

I was utterly stunned to learn I was the first woman he'd brought to Candy's restaurant, especially considering it was obvious he came here often. Astonished didn't begin to capture how I felt. Everything that had transpired over the past twenty-four hours capped with Candy's bits of information had left me flabbergasted and spun sideways inside, scattering my expectations and assumptions like paper in the wind.

Sliding into the booth across from me, Dawson caught my eyes, his narrowing as he took me in. "Are you okay, Evie?"

Ignoring the swirl of emotions inside, I managed to nod. "Sure. Like I told Candy, lunch was delicious. Now take me to the back to meet Red."

Lord knows why I said that. But he said he would, and I was curious to meet someone else who so clearly meant something to him.

Chapter Twelve

DAWSON

Without thinking, I caught Evie's hand in mine as I led her into the back of the restaurant. Once I had her hand in mine, I didn't want to let go. Pushing through the swinging door into the kitchen, I called, "Hey, Red!"

"Dawson, get back here and give me a hug, boy," he called in return.

Red, the closest man I had to a father in spirit, came out from behind the counter. He had a round, sturdy build with twinkling brown eyes and mostly gray hair. He pulled me into a back-slapping hug, forcing me to let go of Evie's hand.

When he drew back, his eyes went right to Evie. "Well, hello there. Candy told me Dawson brought a date today."

Evie smiled politely, and the lines of tension bracketing her mouth and eyes eased. Red's warm and easygoing demeanor had that effect on people. "I'm Evie," she said, holding her hand out.

Red chuckled, reaching his big palm out and engulfing hers. "How was your lunch?" he asked as he dropped her hand.

Pink bloomed on her cheeks, and I wanted to kiss her. "It was heavenly. I'll be coming back, that's for sure."

"Well," Red drawled, "now that Dawson's brought you, I expect you here anytime he is."

Evie's blush deepened.

"Now you know, I'm usually here for work, Red. Evie's not always with me."

Red shrugged easily. "Well, whenever she is, we expect to see you. You been doing okay?"

"Just fine. We should probably go, though. We've got more errands to run for the lodge."

"Just like I have orders to cook. Good to see you. Don't be a stranger. Oh and don't even try to pay for your lunch," he called as I started to turn away.

"Already did," I called back.

"Nice to meet you, Red," Evie said, casting another smile at him.

"You too, darlin'."

When we stepped out of the diner, Evie looked up. "They're so nice. Thank you for bringing me here."

I hadn't thought much about bringing her here, but it suddenly felt meaningful. Candy and Red had known me since I was little and were the closest thing to family I had around here. I'd never even considered bringing another woman here, not even for a casual lunch.

It'd taken me two full years to realize Evie was so much more than just flint to my stone, striking sparks against the desire between us. As she looked up at me, something passed between us. Whether she knew it consciously, I knew she felt that same depth I did. I felt out of my element with her, uncertain what to do with what was happening between us. My only move when it came to women was being a flirt.

I had to play this right with Evie, or I'd screw it all up. I was damn good at letting the people who mattered to me down.

"You're welcome," I replied belatedly. I had to swallow

through the emotion thickening in my throat. Evie squeezed my hand before we turned and walked to my truck.

Hours later, I leaned against my truck's tailgate and looked over at Evie. The sun was setting, the sky above the mountain ridge in the distance a watercolor of lavender, pink, and gold with dusk sliding in to quietly claim the day.

"Good thing we had lunch. At this rate, I'll be starving by the time we unload after we get back to the lodge," I commented.

Evie's return smile was wry. "Sorry I couldn't help with some of the bigger stuff."

"I wasn't saying that to give you a hard time. I like working hard. I'd rather that than stand around waiting for the time to pass. Do you want to eat here before we go or just head back?"

Evie was standing a few feet away from me. When she bit her lip, it felt as if an invisible string cinched tighter between us.

"Here," Evie said softly. "You pick where."

Damn, I wanted to kiss her. With the light turning silvery, her eyes seemed brighter. Her tongue darted out, sliding across her bottom lip. I knew she wasn't trying to be coquettish. Still, I recalled the feel of her tongue slick against mine.

The barest hint of a breeze gusted, shifting the air between us, and I caught a whiff of her scent, spinning around and cinching me a little tighter to her.

When a car door slammed nearby, I took a breath, reminding myself we were only talking about what to get for dinner. Somehow, this felt so much heavier than that. But it was my reaction to her—a wheel rotating, its momentum picking up with each spin, the power of its motion multiplying infinitely.

"You want me to decide where we get dinner?"

She smiled slightly, lifting one shoulder in a tiny shrug.

"Yes. Candy's Diner was so good, I figure you can probably surprise me again."

My heart felt squeezed hard by a fist, all over nothing more than knowing she enjoyed lunch with me.

Because I didn't trust myself to do anything else, I pushed away from the tailgate. "Okay, then." Rounding to the passenger side, I opened the door for her. She stopped with one foot on the running board and glanced up at me. "You're such a gentleman, Dawson."

I shrugged. "My mama taught me manners."

For just a second, I thought she might lean up and kiss me, but she didn't. My eyes landed on the slight pink stain on her cheeks as she turned away and climbed into the truck.

I took her to my second favorite place, yet another fairly nondescript basic place. It was my favorite pub in town. I'd never been much for fancy, maybe because we grew up poor. As far as I could tell, good food was good food, and sometimes fancy places got so full of themselves they messed it all up.

Dinner was largely uneventful. Except for me needing to manage my response to Evie's mere presence. It was crowded when we got there, so we sat at the bar, tucked into a corner. Evie was so close to me that her knee kept bumping into the side of my thigh. Her warm, sweet musky scent spun around me. I didn't drink because we had a bit of a drive.

"You should have a glass of wine," I said at one point.

She held a sweet potato fry between her fingers, right in front of her mouth. Her eyes slid sideways to mine. She popped it in her mouth, and I swallowed at the sight of her pretty lips closing around it.

After she finished chewing, she shook her head. "It's not fair for you to have to drive for an hour and a half while I'm all tipsy."

I shrugged. "I don't mind."

"I do."

She snagged another sweet potato fry from the plate we were sharing, and I wondered how watching her eat could be such a turn-on.

It was fully dark by the time we pulled onto the highway. The drive was quiet at first, and then Evie asked if she could turn on the radio. She scrolled through the stations until the sound of blues filled the truck cab. This woman was going to officially kill me. She loved the blues, maybe as much as I did. Or so I guessed based on how she sighed and leaned into the seat.

We were about halfway back to Stolen Hearts Valley when she spoke between songs. "I need to pee."

"Right now?"

"Yes. Isn't there a rest area maybe a mile ahead or so?"

"Think so. I'll pull over."

Her guess was about spot-on. Not much more than a mile ahead on the highway, the exit sign for a rest area glowed in the darkness. Pulling off the highway, I glanced her way. "I'll go in with you."

She shrugged, hopping out so fast I didn't have a chance to get to the door. I didn't really have to go to the bathroom, but I considered rest areas to be sketchy places. In my father's day, before he passed away, he did many a drug deals at rest areas. As they were transient places with many cars rotating through at just about any hour, it was easier to hide.

I went to the bathroom anyway and waited for Evie right outside the women's room. Moments later, we walked back into the darkness together. A half-moon hung low in the sky above the mountain ridge ahead, its light glinting on Evie's dark hair. She had it in her usual ponytail. I wanted to tug it loose and slide my fingers through the silky fall.

My heart was thudding, and my body felt as if I were standing on the edge of the precipice, tight with anticipation.

After I got the door for Evie and slid into the driver's

side, I sat for a moment. The visceral tug on the invisible string that kept shimmering to life between us had my head turning to look at her. She turned at the same time, and our gaze collided.

The subtle catch of her breath was loud in the quiet. I couldn't help it. I *had* to kiss her.

Leaning over the console, I did exactly as I had imagined moments ago. Lifting a hand, I hooked my finger on the thin elastic holding her hair up and slid it free. The sound of her hair falling down was an audible whoosh in my ears.

"I'm going to kiss you now," I heard myself saying, my voice coming out low and gruff.

It was as if I were waiting to give her a chance to tell me she didn't want to. Not that I'd phrased it as a question. It felt as if sparks were flying in the air around us, the force of the desire so powerful it took on a life of itself.

Evie stared at me, and her breath came out in a little puff. Just when I meant to lean closer, she closed the distance between us, angling toward me. When her lips met mine, the hot joining sent an electric jolt straight through me.

She drew back the barest distance, her lips brushing against mine when she spoke. "Please do."

Cupping her cheek with my fingers teasing in her silky hair, I traced my thumb across her bottom lip. The air was electric at that moment. It felt as if a drum roll were echoing, the need between us burgeoning and increasing in speed and velocity.

I meant to start slowly, and I managed that for maybe five seconds. With a brush of my lips over hers, my thumb slid down, tracing along her jaw and over the wild beat of her pulse as I slipped my hand down to cup the nape of her neck.

When she sighed, a little sound escaped from her throat. It was a lash of the whip in the air between us, sparking a flame into a full-blown conflagration. Angling her head to the side, I fit my mouth over hers and lost myself in her warm, welcoming sweetness. Our kiss went wild, wet, and messy almost instantly.

Evie had this capacity to make me feel like nothing more than a boy. Skill fell to the wayside as I tumbled into everything that was *her*. By the time I drew back, I was gasping for air, my heartbeat thundering so loudly I could barely hear over the sound of blood rushing through my ears.

When Evie's eyes fluttered open, they were unfocused and hazy. Although the lights from the parking lot were dim, I could still see the pink on her flushed cheeks. Her lips were puffy from our kiss. My need for her pounded through my body. *All* I wanted was to kiss her again.

So I did. I dove right back into the fire. God, I loved the way she kissed—her mouth lush and mobile and her tongue darting in to lick against mine. She took little nips on my bottom lip. Over and over again, those soft little sounds from the back of her throat made me fucking crazy.

Restless and aching down to my bones to have her closer, I reached over and tugged her onto my lap. Our kiss broke apart as she shifted, her knee catching on the console between us. The little giggle that escaped from her was another lash of the whip on my need. She settled in my lap, leaning against the steering wheel with a small smile curling her lips.

She rocked her hips slightly as she settled down over my arousal, making me acutely aware of how hard I was and how much I needed her. Her smile faded as we stared at each other with my heart kicking hard inside the cage of my ribs.

"What are we doing?" she asked, her voice raspy.

I pressed a kiss just above the point where the collar of her shirt dipped down above her breasts. "Kissing," I murmured.

I leaned back, giving in to the need to feel more of her. I slid my hand under her shirt, encountering her warm skin and savoring the soft little sigh that escaped her lips.

"And this," I murmured as I slid my palm up, lightly cupping one of her breasts. I could feel the nipple puckering under the silk. As aroused as I was—and let's face it, I wanted to be buried deep inside her—all I wanted was to give her pleasure.

For a man accustomed to approaching sex as a transaction, the way I felt with Evie was unfamiliar and disorienting. As intense and potentially fraught with emotional implications as it was, I didn't shy away from it.

My need for her was too fierce and overpowering.

"Dawson," she gasped when I caught her tight nipple between my thumb and forefinger and squeezed lightly.

"Just let me take care of you."

When I looked into her eyes, I saw surprise and recognized the uncertainty flickering there. Sliding her shirt up, I flicked the clasp loose between her breasts and groaned aloud at the lush weight of her breasts and the feel of her silky skin.

Dipping my head, I sucked one of her sweet, pink nipples into my mouth. Her hips rocked over the hard ridge of my cock, and she let out a little whimper.

Evie was a fan of leggings and conveniently wore a pair today. They were soft and stretchy. After taking a moment to give her sweet ass a squeeze, I shimmied my hand down into the front of her panties. She was hot and slick, her channel rippling around my fingers when I sank two inside her.

She gasped, leaning forward and pressing a messy kiss on the side of my neck. With her hips rolling slightly as I teased around her clit and fucked her hot pussy with my fingers, I wanted to see her fly apart so badly. Nothing about this was for me, well, except for the fact that it mattered so much to me that she found her release.

Evie lifted her head, her blue eyes glittering in the darkness when she arched into my fingers. "Dawson," she gasped, the frayed sound of her voice sending a hot jolt straight to my balls. "I want you inside me."

Her words were blunt and direct, cinching me tighter and tighter to her. Circling my thumb, I drew my fingers out, watching her face. She bit her lip, a low moan escaping and her eyes on me the whole time.

"This isn't exactly the best place for that," I choked out when she pressed down over my arousal.

Her lips curled in a slight smile. "This isn't exactly the best place for what we're already doing."

Just when I thought I had the situation in hand, she shifted her hips back slightly. With a quick flick, she had my fly unbuttoned and was curling her hand around my cock.

My head fell back. "Evie..." I growled.

I felt her shifting and opened my eyes to see her kick one leg free from her leggings and rise up over me. Her slick heat slid over my shaft, her wet core teasing the tip.

"Fuck, Evie. I need a condom."

Her eyes widened slightly, but I was already moving, reaching for my wallet. She shook her head. "Didn't we already discuss this? I'm on the pill." She gasped as she rocked her hips again, the slick kiss of her pussy on the head of my cock nearly undoing me.

Holding still, I eyed her, recalling we had, in fact, had this chat in the early morning hours. When she bit her lip, I nodded, gripping her hips as she rose. With a slow slide, she brought me inside her, sheathing me in her core.

This was messy and intense and out of my control. It certainly wasn't what I had planned. But then, Evie had a hold on me so tight I wasn't letting go.

When she settled down fully, burying me all the way inside, she gave her hips a little rock, nearly drawing my release from me with nothing more than that. Tightening my grip on her hips, I held her still. "Slow down."

Opening my eyes, I brushed her tangled hair away from her face, and her forehead fell to mine. For several breaths, we held still. Fused together, our hearts pounded. A sense of intimacy fell over me, a closeness I'd never experienced with anyone before. I swallowed, sliding one arm around her waist to pull her closer.

She shifted slightly, murmuring against my lips, "I can't help it."

The moments that followed felt like the most intense in my life. There on the side of the highway, we made love in the darkness in my truck. Every rock of my hips into her sent pleasure streaking through me, my balls tightening and electricity humming at the base of my spine.

I felt her release coming, the ripples of her channel increasing in intensity and those little sounds in her throat pushing me closer to my own release. She came hard, her entire body shuddering roughly as her pussy clamped down around my cock. Her head fell to my shoulder as my own release came abruptly, my mouth hot on her neck as I moaned her name.

We stayed fused for several long moments with nothing but the sound of our breathing filling the space. Headlights flashed across us, and she lifted her head quickly.

Before she moved away, I cupped her cheek and looked into her eyes for a long moment. My heart was about to beat its way out of my chest.

I didn't know what to say, so I simply leaned forward to press a kiss on her lips. When another pair of headlights flashed through the parking area, she smiled softly. "I suppose we should keep driving."

We drove home through the darkness. All the while, one word beat like a drum in my brain. *Mine. Mine. Mine.*

Chapter Thirteen

EVIE

"Come to bed with me."

Nothing but a little slice of moonlight falling through the trees illuminated Dawson's face. His face, so beautiful anyway, was all strong angles in the shadows.

I opened my mouth to reply, and he squeezed my hand. "Just to sleep," he clarified.

With my body still humming with tiny aftershocks from our heated encounter in his truck, I found I didn't want to leave him. My emotions were a muddle, but the idea of sleeping wrapped up in Dawson's strong embrace was too good and far too tempting for me to resist.

As soon as I even began to nod, he smiled. Turning and keeping my hand tightly held in his, he led me along the path, following the lights strung through the trees to his cabin.

That was how I found myself falling asleep enveloped in his arms once again. I didn't know what to do with any of my feelings, yet all my worries fell to the wayside when he pulled me against him and curled around me. I fell asleep almost instantly.

Close to a week later, I leaned against Dani's desk, looking down at the schedule she had in front of us. She tapped her finger on an upcoming weekend a few weeks ahead. "With Grace out of town, do you mind doing two shifts on this Saturday?" she asked.

I shook my head. "Of course, I don't mind."

She jotted my name down on the calendar before sticking the pencil through the bun barely contained on top of her head. Several of her wild brown curls were springing out.

"So what's up with you and Dawson?"

My mouth actually fell open.

Dani laughed. "You don't think any of us have noticed? I promise, I don't keep an eye on who sleeps where, but I'm up early."

I sank down into the chair across from her desk and cast her a glare. "So you don't pay attention to who sleeps where, but you have some sort of opinion about where I sleep?"

Dani cocked her head to the side, a grin teasing the corners of her mouth. "I leave to come into the restaurant at five thirty most mornings. I might've noticed twice now that Dawson was leaving your place. The other morning, I saw you leaving Dawson's place. And I'm nosy."

I couldn't help but smile at that. Dani *was* nosy, but she also cared, and she didn't tend to spread gossip. She always went straight to the source. In this case, I supposed that was me.

"I don't know what's going on," I said, reaching for a rubber band in front of me on her desk. I needed something to fiddle with, so I stretched it between my fingers, snapping it lightly.

"I need a little more information than that to give you any advice," Dani replied.

I rolled my eyes. "Fine. So he kissed me. It was kind of

out of the blue a couple of weeks ago. You know, at the fundraiser when I ended up with wine spilled all over my dress after that woman bumped into me?" At Dani's nod, I continued. "Dawson gave me a ride home and kissed me. Then we ran into each other one night up at that flat rock." She looked puzzled. "There's no path to it, and you have to cut through the trees behind his cabin."

"Oh, right. Got it. I hardly ever go there."

"Anyway, he kissed me again." I stopped there, not wanting to elaborate on how much more had happened. Because there was *more*.

Dani was quiet, her gaze shifting from a teasing look to considering. After a moment, she said, "It's always been obvious to me that you two really liked each other."

"It has?" I stopped fiddling with the rubber band and stared at her.

Her brows hitched up. "Seriously. I mean, sure, Dawson teases everyone, but you have a special place. With you, he's always been like a little boy picking on the girl he likes in first grade."

I laughed and sighed. "But I don't know what the hell we're doing. He says he wants to take it one step at a time. I confronted him and asked him point blank if he was going to screw around, and he assured me he wasn't."

"Dawson's more of a flirt than a player. He's good at creating an impression, but—" She paused and shrugged.

"But what?"

"Just that. He loves to flirt. And sure, he might be a fan of no-strings sex, but he doesn't get around as much as I think people think he does."

I had *so* many questions but elected to keep them to myself. I was confused enough about my own feelings and why I was even letting this play out. Except for the times when I was tangled up in Dawson and caught up in the rush of desire between us, doubts crowded out almost everything else in my mind.

Back in high school, when I was having a hard time after my twin sister died, and I truly felt as if half of me was dead, I was the awkward one. While everyone else focused on fun, I felt out of place, insecure, and sad. That girl still lived inside my heart, always ready to remind me that guys like Dawson—handsome, sexy, teasing, and popular—couldn't be interested in me.

Plenty of time had passed, yet the aftereffects of those formative years were hard to shake loose. I was definitely getting the sense that I hadn't looked past the surface with Dawson.

Dani's phone rang, but she didn't answer. After another lengthy pause, she drummed her fingers on the desk. "Dawson's a nice guy," she said softly. "He's been through some stuff."

"Huh? What do you mean?"

The phone stopped ringing. "That's for him to tell you."

"Dani! You're my friend. This is a girl thing. You have to tell me something."

Dani bit her lip, looking conflicted. "I know, but he's actually a pretty private person. You might as well ask him about his family, seeing as you two are getting close."

Her phone started ringing again. This time, her eyes flicked over to look at it. "It's Jackson. I should get it."

"Fine. I need to go anyway."

Standing, I gave a little wave as I turned to leave her office. Slipping the rubber band over my wrist, I snapped it lightly as I walked down the hall, wondering just what Dawson had been through.

The night I found him up at the rock, I'd sensed something was bothering him, but he didn't let on to whatever it was. He'd been gone for three days now on a guided hike through the mountains.

I missed him.

Chapter Fourteen

DAWSON

I leaned back in my chair, rolling my shoulders in a futile attempt to ease the tension bundled there. Jackson caught my eye, and I sensed his concern, so I looked away. I wasn't up for Jackson trying to read my mood because it wasn't great.

I would always be thankful Candy had told me about this job. I'd needed something to get me out of my hometown. Between working at the lodge and being on the first responder team, the variety kept me from feeling restless. The team here was rock solid.

Sometimes I wondered if I needed to dance along the edge of risk to keep me sane. I respected the hell out of Jackson. He was a good guy and a great boss. Every now and then, though, his perceptiveness grated on me. He knew that night still bothered me. I suspected he knew why even though we'd never had a specific conversation about it.

I kicked those thoughts to the curb and focused on the training. By late afternoon, Jackson and I were the first people on the Stolen Hearts Valley Emergency Response Team trained to administer naloxone on-site when we responded to opioid overdose calls. It was our best hope to stem the tide of accidental deaths occurring at a shocking rate across America. The rest of the crew would rotate through the training over the next two weeks.

After we climbed into Jackson's truck, his gaze slid sideways. "Lunch?"

"Of course. I'm fucking starving."

"Any requests?"

"Candy's Diner if I get to pick."

Although Evie was the first woman I'd ever brought to Candy's, whenever I came to Asheville with any of the guys, I always suggested it. Not only was the food fucking awesome, but I also wanted to give Candy the business. Even though she wasn't hurting for it.

Jackson flashed a grin. "As if I would say no to Candy's. That was going to be my suggestion, anyway."

I chuckled as he started the engine and rolled out of the parking lot. We were on the far side of town, and the first few minutes of the drive were quiet. Jackson finally spoke, going straight to the heart of the matter.

"I know that night still bothers you. Wanna talk about it?"

"Uh, no."

I was staring out the window, but I could feel Jackson's eyes shift my way. "Well, you gave me a kick in the ass about Shay more than once, so I'm going to return the favor. The guy's fine. Sometimes we're going to run into stuff that might hit too close to home."

I closed my eyes, taking a deep breath and letting it out slowly. "I know that, man. I guess I can stop wondering if you know what happened to my dad."

"Dude, I am *not* trying to lecture you about any of it. I've seen my own share of stuff that comes back to haunt me every now and then."

The tension that had started to tighten in my chest eased slightly. "I know. I'm fine. I guess it's good that the first time

I had a call that was almost a fucking repeat of what happened to my dad, the guy survived. Sometimes, they won't."

"Yeah, and sometimes we're not gonna be the first people there. That was a fluke."

"It fucking sucks. You know?"

"Yeah, I do know. This opioid shit is insane. Never seen anything like it."

"It pisses me off. Because I don't think my dad was trying to kill himself. That shit kills people too easily."

"Exactly."

Quiet filled the space again, and I was relieved Jackson didn't feel the need to say more. He was a good friend, and he knew when to let things stay quiet.

"Just so you know, I'm okay. It did get to me, but I'm okay."

"Good to know. If you ever need to talk, I'm here."

Candy paused beside our booth, glancing back and forth between Jackson and me. "You boys all done?"

"Yes, ma'am," Jackson replied with a wink. "I could use a top off for my coffee, though."

Candy quickly refilled both of our coffees. "Where's the bill?" I asked as she began to turn away when another customer lifted their coffee mug to get her attention.

"There is no bill."

"Candy, I swear—" I began.

She waved me off with a laugh. "That's the only way I can keep you from paying."

"Still won't work," I called.

Jackson took a few swallows of coffee before saying, "I'm gonna use the men's room. I'll be back in a few."

After he walked off, I nursed my coffee while Evie sashayed straight into my thoughts. It had been four long days since I'd seen her. I'd led a three-day hiking trip into the mountains before Jackson and I met in Asheville for this first round of training. I was beyond ready to get back to the lodge and see her.

The problem was, we hadn't defined anything between us. I knew what I wanted, and I didn't care if it was crazy. I just didn't quite know how to sweet-talk Evie into realizing it.

"So where's your girlfriend?"

Candy's voice nudged me out of my thoughts, and I glanced up. "Well, she's obviously not here."

"Smartass," she parried with a grin.

I shrugged. "Just finished leading a hiking trip, and Jackson met me here for the training. Trust me, I'd love for her to be here with me."

Candy was quiet for a moment, the teasing glint fading in her eyes. "You really like her."

"I do."

Her smile unfurled slowly. "I thought so. I think she really likes you too."

"I sure hope so. She might not have the best impression of me, though."

Candy rolled her eyes and sighed. "Right. Because you're Mr. Flirt-with-everyone routine might bite you in the ass. Far as I can tell, Evie is giving you the benefit of the doubt, so you'll just have to show her who you really are. You heard from your mama?" she asked, shifting topics quickly.

I took a slow breath and nodded. "We talk every few weeks at least."

Candy's gaze became somber. "Make sure you take time to go see her, okay? I had my reasons for telling you about that job. I knew you needed to escape the long ass shadow your dad cast over you, but your mama loves you."

My throat tightened, and I took a sip of coffee, swallowing through the pain. "I know she does. And I love her.

Don't worry. I make sure to get there to see her every few months."

Jackson came out of the restroom, striding toward us. Candy turned when he reached the table. "Always good to see you, Jackson. I need to get into the kitchen. I've got orders to serve," she said as a little bell rang from the back.

Jackson leaned over and kissed her on the cheek. "Thanks for lunch, Candy."

Candy gave me just enough time to give her a quick hug before hurrying off. I walked beside Jackson on the way out. "We're paying something, right?" he asked as I paused by the register.

"Oh, hell yeah. I stuff money in the cash drawer when she tries to keep me from paying." Chuckling, I leaned over the counter and popped open the drawer, dropping in two fifty-dollar bills.

I ignored Candy calling after us as we walked through the door.

A shaft of moonlight fell across the bed, illuminating the bare curve of Evie's shoulder in the darkness. My breath came in heaves, and my skin was slick with sweat. Evie was warm and soft against my side. I could feel the point of one of her nipples pressing into me, and that alone sent another jolt of desire through me.

I could *not* fucking get enough of her.

Luck had shined down on me after I got back to the lodge. When I was walking through the trees, I saw her up ahead and caught up to her right quick.

The moment she turned, and said, "Hey, Dawson," I'd kissed her.

My heartbeat gradually slowed, and I fell asleep tangled up with her.

Hours later, I felt her shift against me and opened my

eyes. Sunshine fell at an angle across the bed in a splash of white-gold light.

Evie's blue eyes blinked open. After a moment, she cleared her throat. "Good morning." Her voice was soft and frayed from sleep.

I sifted my fingers through her silky hair, enjoying the subtle sensation of it sliding through my fingers. Although my cock stirred to life and I wanted her with a piercing need, I was quite content to simply rest here with her.

I was beginning to realize I'd missed out with my stupid rule to never sleep with a woman. Although, deep in the corner of my mind, I knew it was specific to Evie. Waking up like this with anyone else held no appeal.

"Mornin'," I replied, my voice coming out raspy.

Evie rose on her elbow, glancing at the clock on the nightstand beside my bed. My eyes followed hers to see it was not quite seven a.m.

"Are you working this weekend?" I asked.

Evie's gaze slid back to mine as she shook her head.

"I need to go to the coast for a few days, and I was wondering if you wanted to go with me."

My words strolled out before I thought them through. At all. Taking Evie with me to visit my family was fraught with potential complications, but instead of dwelling, I dismissed them all in my mind.

Evie's eyes widened slightly, a subtle flush cresting on her cheekbones. I could feel her heartbeat kick up slightly. She was resting against my chest, and I felt it thudding hard and fast against my ribs.

"Sure," she replied slowly.

Since I didn't have words for how good it felt that she said yes, I leaned forward slightly and pressed my lips to hers.

When I drew back, her flush deepened, and she announced, "I have to pee."

Grinning, I loosened my hold, and she slipped out of

bed. A moment later, I heard the toilet flush and rolled over to see her walking back. Evie was a sight. Her dark hair was mussed, and her body a little flushed with the imprint of the sheets on her skin. When her crooked smile unfurled, my heart gave a resounding thump.

"When are we leaving?" she asked.

"As soon as we get ready."

"I'm gonna hop in the shower then."

She turned, giving me a nice view of her delectable ass. I swung my feet to the floor and followed her into the bathroom. She had already turned on the shower, and steam was filling the room.

When I stepped in the bathroom, Evie glanced over. "I'm joining you in the shower," I explained.

She shrugged and slid the curtain back to step inside. This was another first for me. With my unspoken rule of not sleeping with anyone, I'd never showered with a woman.

The moment I was in there with her, all I wanted was her. A wet, soapy Evie was a temptation unlike any I'd ever encountered. Stepping in front of her, I slid my hands down over her bubbly sides. Her eyes opened, and she sputtered slightly, lifting her head.

"Dawson ..."

"Mmmhmm?" I murmured as I dipped my head, pressing a kiss on her shoulder and sliding my tongue along her collarbone before making my way to her breasts.

"If we're driving to the coast," she began, pausing with a gasp when I sucked one of her sweet nipples into my mouth. I let it go with a light pop. She continued on the heels of a low moan. "Don't you think we should go soon?"

I lifted my head, brushing a kiss over her lips. "We can make this quick," I replied against her mouth, loving that I could feel the curve of her smile.

Reaching between her thighs, I found her hot and slick. Turning, I shifted her back so she was against the wall and slightly out of the water raining down around us. Lifting her against me, I loved how easily her legs curled around my hips. I didn't know what it was about Evie, but she just did it for me. In every way.

I let my cock slide through her slick folds, watching her face as her head fell with a thump against the tile. She bit her lip as a little cry escaped.

As I started to draw away, she squeezed her legs tighter. "Oh, no," she said, her eyes flying open, "you don't get to tease me like that and then go away."

My chuckle turned into a groan when she rocked against me. Water rained down against our legs. With Evie wrapped around me, my heart squeezed hard. "Just trying not to rush too much," I said, gritting my teeth to hang onto my control when I felt her soaked pussy glide over my cock again.

"Please," she gasped. "Don't make me wait."

Whatever Evie wanted, she got. Easing back slightly, I adjusted the angle of my hips, the thick crown of my cock pressing against her entrance. For a beat, we both held our breath, and then I slowly slid inside her. I let out a groan, my forehead falling to hers.

She felt so good, so slick and snug, a silken sheath around my cock. She shifted her hips just barely, rocking into me. It was fast and messy for several deep strokes, and then her pussy was clenching around me, and my release poured into her. I came with a rough cry, my mouth hot and open on her neck as I held on tight.

Afterward, we actually used the shower for its intended purpose. I walked with Evie over to her cabin while she got some clothes together for the weekend. As she slung her backpack over her shoulder, she caught my eye. "Dani knows about us."

I shrugged. "Were we keeping it a secret?"

Evie's cheeks flushed pretty and pink, and she rolled her eyes. "I don't know. I don't know what this is, and now you're taking me somewhere for the weekend."

I sensed her confusion, and I wanted to tell her not to be confused.

You're mine was what I wanted to say.

But I sensed that might be pushing things too far and too fast. As certain as I was about my feelings for her, I was equally certain that I was no expert at navigating the tricky terrain of a relationship and anything that involved the heart.

One step at a time was what I told myself.

"I need to let Dani know I'll be gone for the weekend just so she doesn't try to call me in for any shifts. Seeing as she'll know we'll be gone together, that means everyone's going to know something," she explained, her cheeks getting brighter with every word.

"Okay. You just tell me what to say."

Evie sighed and grumbled something under her breath as she eyed my backpack. "You have hardly anything."

"Three T-shirts and three pairs of jeans," I said with a chuckle.

Evie twisted her lips to the side as she stuffed a few more things into her quite full backpack. As we walked out, she glanced over. "I'm just going to text Dani."

Not much later, she rode beside me in my truck with her gaze aimed out the window as we drove through the mountains. I didn't quite know what prompted me to invite her to come with me, but I knew with certainty I wanted her right here with me.

Chapter Fifteen

EVIE

Dawson's brother, Chad, stared at me, his gaze considering. "Nice to meet you."

Chad looked remarkably like Dawson, albeit a younger, less hardened version. I couldn't believe I was even considering Dawson hard, but as I'd gotten to know him, I'd learned there was an edge. His brother was softer, his humor less of a reflex.

"You too," I replied.

Looking around, I took in the space. We were in a big square building, some sort of a construction worksite. Chad brushed an unruly lock of blond hair out of his eyes; a gesture that reminded me a little bit of Dawson. "Do you want to grab some dinner?"

"Of course. We're here for the weekend."

Chad cracked a smile. "Mom know you're coming?"

"Yeah. I texted her. How's she doing?"

The undercurrents were running strong and fast here, and I didn't know how to read them.

Chad shrugged. "She's okay. She's comfortable, and I

suppose that's all that matters. How about we go see her first?"

I sensed a slight hesitation in Dawson, but he nodded, his gaze level and a subtle tension gathering at the corners of his eyes and mouth. "Sounds good to me. You need to go home first?"

Chad held Dawson's eyes for a long moment, some kind of silent communication occurring, then he nodded. "Yeah, I'll grab a shower. Where are you staying?"

"I booked a room at Dune's Beach."

If it was unusual for Dawson not to stay with his family, it didn't show on Chad's face. He nodded his assent and turned away from us. He quickly tidied up the area where he'd been working, sweeping up some sawdust and dumping it in the trashcan before putting away his tools.

"What do you have going these days for projects?" Dawson asked conversationally.

"Oh, we're working on several houses in a new subdivision. I'm doing the cabinetry work right now." Chad closed the case over a power tool and turned to face us. "Let's go."

Moments later, I watched Chad's truck turn the opposite direction on the road. The blinker in Dawson's truck clicked in the background as he waited for a car to pass on the road. "Not to be weird, but do you usually stay at a hotel when you visit your family?" I asked.

Dawson didn't turn to look toward me. His hand had been relaxed over the top of the steering wheel, but at my words, his fingers curled around it, gripping tightly. I could almost feel the ripple of tension run through him, and I suddenly regretted my question.

"I guess I might as well give you a little background. No, I don't stay with my family. My brother's got his own place, an apartment above the main offices for his construction company. He took over the company after our dad died. My mom is in an assisted living home. She has emphysema and congestive heart failure. Not because she smoked, but probably because she spent too long sucking up the secondhand smoke from my father. She helps Chad with the accounting, but she doesn't get out much. We still have the old family home."

He tacked on that last sentence almost as an afterthought.

"Oh, how come your brother doesn't live there?"

Dawson hadn't pulled out and seemed to have forgotten we were driving anywhere. He finally looked my way, his silvery-gray gaze holding mine. Looking into his eyes, I felt as if I were watching clouds gathering in the sky.

"I hate that house. It's not something I like to talk much about, but my dad was a fucking asshole. He knocked me and my mom around. He was a drunk, and then he got hooked on pills. He died there. If the house were in my name, I'd have sold it already, but it's up to my mom and my brother." He recited that brief history in a flat, weary tone. A jagged silence fell, and he released the steering wheel, running his hand through his hair and letting it fall to the seat where his fingers idly traced along a row of stitching.

It felt as if a brick had hit me in the chest, the weight of those few sentences was so heavy. "Oh my God. I'm so sorry, Dawson. I had no idea."

My words felt entirely inadequate. I wanted to be able to reach into the past and somehow protect Dawson. Instinctively, I reached for his hand, curling mine around it.

His eyes slid away, his lashes sweeping against his cheeks as he closed them. Not that I hadn't already caught on, but I was becoming more keenly aware of just how little I knew about Dawson.

When his eyes swept open again, the pain and regret there had tears stinging hot at the backs of my eyes. Yet it didn't seem right for me to be the one crying. I waited, sensing he had more to say.

The sound of him swallowing was audible in the small cab of the truck. "Yeah, it sucked. I love my mom, and my brother means the world to me, but I gotta love them from a distance. Being here brings up too much shit for me." His fingers tightened around mine, giving a little squeeze. "I don't know why I wanted to bring you here. I didn't mean for it to be weird."

My heart felt cracked open, the depth of emotion I felt for Dawson multiplying the more my understanding of him expanded.

"It's not weird. Family is messy. My parents were loving, and nothing like that happened, but they were also kind of strict and pretty overprotective, especially after my sister died. So don't ever apologize for stuff like that. We all have messed up stuff with our families."

His eyes held mine, and the intent and searching look contained within them stripped me bare.

"Okay," he said, his voice low and gruff. He leaned forward, surprising me when he pressed his lips to mine. The kiss was brief, and there was nothing sexual about it, but it tugged on my heart, stitching me tighter to him.

He leaned back, squeezing my hand again before he released it. He looked forward, watching as another car passed us by. When he turned onto the main road, he glanced sideways. "Dune's Beach is nice, by the way. It's where I usually stay. Maybe because when I was a kid, it was so far above my life, but now I can afford it. I might not be rich, but I'm sure as hell not as poor as I once was."

"It seems like your brother does all right," I commented.

"He's done real well for himself, taking what my dad left behind and making it better."

We fell quiet after that. I looked out the window, watching the flat landscape unfurl. Half a day's drive later, the mountains had given way to rolling hills about midway through the state before the land leveled to the coastal plains of North Carolina. We were driving on a highway along the beach. All the signs of the crowded coastal world were apparent with neon signs and shops everywhere. It was far less busy than when I'd been here in years past. I'd come here a few times in the summers with my family, and it was always packed to the gills with cars and people.

With it being autumn, the crowds had thinned, and the beaches were empty except for a few walkers. The wind whipped across the Atlantic Ocean, and tangerine and gold streaked the sky as the sun slid down the horizon opposite the sea.

"Unlike my dad, Chad stays sober and works his ass off. There's good money in construction when you do that. I love to build, but there was no way I would take over my dad's business," Dawson added, his low voice piercing the quiet.

"I understand," I said softly, my heart aching to think about what Dawson's childhood must've been like. I had only a sketch of the details, but I felt the echo of the pain he carried.

The rest of the drive was quiet, but it was comfortable. I was coming to learn silence with Dawson was usually comfortable. I liked that about him and us. I was starting to realize that my heart was in *real* danger here.

I didn't suppose one step at a time meant my step being a stumble and fall into love.

———

Dawson's mother was lovely. I knew at a glance that his beautiful silver-gray eyes and the almost aristocratic bent to his features came from her. She had the same lovely cheekbones and strong nose. Her fading blond hair was tied up in a knot. She managed to be elegant even though she was on oxygen.

She patted the chair beside her, her eyes on Dawson. "Now, honey. Come sit by me."

I wasn't sure how to manage this, but Dawson said he wanted me to meet her. I'd had manners drilled into me by my mother, so I figured they would get me through this. Here I was, well on the way into being in love with her son with no idea how he felt about me, nor how she would interpret my presence with him.

When Dawson reached her chair, he leaned over to press a gentle kiss against her temple. "How ya feelin'?"

Her voice was reedy when she spoke. "I'm all right. I miss you," she said as he sat gingerly in the chair beside her.

He squeezed her hand. "Love you, Mom. Came to visit because I miss you."

The love and affection between them were so clear, it almost hurt to bear witness to it. Dawson glanced over at me. "I brought someone to meet you. This is Evie," he said with a nod in my direction. "And this is my mother, Anita."

His mother looked over at me, her smile warm. "Well, hello, dear. Dawson has never brought a girl to visit me, so you must be special."

I smiled. "I didn't know that. Now I'm kind of nervous," I said honestly. "But it's quite nice to meet you."

Anita angled her head to the chair on her other side. I sat down, perching on the edge of the seat and folding my hands on my knees.

"So tell me about yourself."

Her words were kind, but I had no idea where to start. I suppose when you visit someone sick, the likelihood they would cut through the bullshit was much higher. I imagine she didn't want to waste time with small talk.

"Well, I'm Evie," I began, immediately wondering why I repeated the introduction. "I met Dawson because we both work at Stolen Hearts Lodge. I grew up near there." Pausing, I looked at Dawson. I could see his expression was careful. Strangely, it gave me a sense of relief to realize this was possibly as new to him as it was to me. We hadn't done the meeting the family thing, so it was new for both of us.

Just as I was wondering what else to say, Chad arrived, taking the focus off me. I leaned back and mostly listened as they chatted. By the time we left, the tension had unspooled slightly inside me. His mother pulled me close for a hug when she stood, moving her oxygen out of the way on its wheeled cart.

A short drive later, we were at a seafood restaurant with a lovely view of the ocean in the downstairs of our hotel.

"So, Evie, tell me how you and Dawson met," Chad said after we had ordered.

Dawson rolled his eyes. "Dude, you already know that. How about you tell me what's up with your love life?" he parried, kicking the can of the conversation right back to him.

Chad chuckled. "Dude, I'm six years younger than you, and I'm running a business. I don't have time for romance."

Dawson threw his head back with a laugh. "Fair enough."

They settled into an easy banter. Once his brother wasn't questioning me about the status of our relationship, I discovered he had the same easygoing humor as Dawson. Only at one point did something tense come up.

Chad commented, "So we need to talk about the house. Mom signed over her half to you. I'd like to put it on the market and unload it once and for all."

"What the fuck?" Dawson muttered. His hand tightened around the beer bottle he held. "Look, man, I told her I wanted nothing to do with it. I don't want the money."

"Yeah, and she pointed out she's fucking dying," Chad retorted. "I don't wanna argue with her about it. She did it behind my back. I'm assuming you're on board with me putting it on the market?"

"Of course. I don't want the money."

"Let's worry about that when we sell it."

Dawson stood abruptly from the booth. "Be right back. I'm running to the men's room."

After he strode away quickly, I looked over at Chad and shrugged. "That seems like a touchy subject."

Chad sighed, running a hand through his hair and leaning back. "Oh, hell yeah. What do you know?"

"Not much. Just that your dad knocked y'all around, and then he died of an overdose."

Chad was quiet for several moments, looking down at the table and tracing his fingertip along with the lines of a pattern on the placemat. On the heels of a deep breath, he lifted his head, lasering me with his eyes. "Look, Dawson is one of the best men I know. He took care of me when we were growing up. My father never laid a hand on me because Dawson always got in the way. I can tell things might be fresh between you two, but you gotta understand it's fucking *huge* that he brought you here."

My mouth almost dropped open as I stared at him. Meanwhile, my heart ached a little more for the boy who'd protected his own younger brother so completely.

"Oh," I breathed, swallowing through the emotion tightening in my throat.

Chad smiled, a touch of sadness and rue contained in his gaze. "Maybe I'm overstepping, but I wanted to say something because it seems like you really like him. I also know how my big brother can come across."

"What do you mean?"

"The class clown. That's how he covers up. He's funny as hell, so it comes easy. He's also a relentless flirt, which I'm sure you know."

I laughed softly, pausing to finish off my glass of wine. "I might be familiar with that tendency of his."

At that moment, Dawson returned to the table, sliding into the booth beside me. Glancing at his brother, he asked, "So why don't you just decide what the plan will be with the house and let me know?"

Tension emanated from Dawson. His eyes were guarded, his lips pressed in a thin line, and his shoulders were stiff. I wanted to hug him close and tell him not to worry, but now wasn't the time for that.

"No problem," Chad said easily. "I was already dealing with it anyway. I just didn't want you to get surprised if you got something in the mail about it since Mom signed over her portion to you."

Dawson nodded tightly. "Thanks, man." After a beat, he shifted topics. "You going to get out to the mountains to visit me any day?"

Chad flashed a grin. "In all my spare time."

A smile teased the corners of Dawson's mouth, and I could sense him relaxing a little. "It wouldn't do you any harm to take a break."

"I'll think about it. Maybe come summer when it's so fucking hot here I could use a few days away from the construction sites."

Chad deftly moved the conversation onto lighter matters after that, sharing a few funny stories from local friends. By the time we left to go to the room, Dawson was relaxed again. He insisted on covering the bill, giving his brother a back-slapping hug before we left. "Breakfast tomorrow?"

"Of course. Should I just meet y'all here?"

"No, let's grab breakfast at Candy's old diner. She tells me it's still good," Dawson replied.

When Chad nodded, Dawson smiled, sliding his arm around my shoulders as his brother turned away with a wave. When he glanced down at me, I thought I still saw a glimmer of pain in his gaze. My heart gave a little squeeze, and I wanted to pull him close and remind him that pain was just something you had to learn to live with sometimes. I sensed he knew it already, but he tried so damn hard not to dwell.

While I couldn't say I had the same experiences—because none of us shared the same life—when my sister died, I truly felt as if a part of me was ripped away. In a way, it was. She was my identical twin, and that kind of bond wasn't something I'd ever find again. Even in the face of what felt insurmountable at first, the gaping wound in my heart had eventually scabbed over and healed.

Scars are tougher than unblemished skin. Even those invisible scars we carry on our hearts. Those become the strongest of all. Because you learn you can walk through the fire and come out stronger on the other side. You might actually get burned, but you'd still be okay and be all the tougher for it.

Dawson's hand slipped from my shoulder and along the curve of my waist to rest on my hip. Pausing beside the elevator, he glanced down again and promptly stole my breath, sending butterflies aflutter in my belly. The look in his eyes was dark and intent, barely leashed desire.

Chapter Sixteen

DAWSON

I could feel the soft give of Evie's skin under my palm. I was wound tight inside. Although her presence here added to my sense of confusion, I was beyond relieved she was here.

I tried to visit every few months, yet the ghosts of the past were always waiting for me. I hated that my mother was sick. I knew death was a foregone conclusion for all of us, but it didn't seem fair for her to be sick.

She'd put up with too much fucking bullshit and pain doled out by my father—sometimes with his fists and sometimes with emotional cuts. After he died, all I wanted for her was an easy life. Every spare penny I had went into covering her long-term care insurance, which wasn't cheap. I just wanted her to be comfortable.

And that fucking house? I wanted nothing to do with it and no profit from it. I'd already decided I would simply sign it over to my brother.

Evie's presence was like a beam of sunshine. Her warm smile and the promise contained in her gorgeous blue eyes eased the coldness that could so easily descend over me whenever I came home.

Once we were in the elevator, I leaned against the wall and pulled her close. She didn't hesitate, her soft curves pressing against me. She'd become so much more than a distraction. She didn't know it yet, but she fucking owned me. And I had no idea how to play this, to get her to see how much she mattered to me.

How much *we* mattered.

For tonight, I would lose myself in her.

I brushed her silky hair away from her face, watching her eyes darken slightly, and her tongue dart out to moisten her lips.

"Thanks for coming with me. I suppose I should've warned you," I said.

"About what? Your brother's a nice guy, and your mom is a sweetheart. I'm sorry she's sick."

My chest felt tight, and I ignored the voice that wanted to tell me I didn't deserve someone like Evie. Because this girl? She just did it for me.

Here she was, being sweet, even though I got all pissed at my brother about our childhood home.

"I got a little cranky back there," I explained with a shrug.

"It's okay. I don't blame you. We all have stuff we have to carry."

She leaned up and pressed her lips to mine. I thought she meant the kiss to comfort me, but as spun tight as I was inside, it instantly morphed into the fiery desire burning between us. When I was close to Evie, the heat was always banked, so all it took was the slightest bit of fuel. Her lips on mine were more than a little bit.

I slipped one hand into her hair, cupping the nape of her neck with the other gliding down her back to squeeze her sweet, lush ass. She dived right into the flames with me, opening her mouth on a sigh.

Moments later, we were both gasping for air when the elevator stopped. Stumbling out, I held her hand tightly in mine. She hurried down the hall with me through the door into our room.

Kicking the door shut behind me with my boot, I spun her around, and we slammed against the wall in the narrow entryway. Our kiss was hot and messy. I devoured her mouth, and she met me stroke for stroke, never once hesitating, never once backing down.

I tugged at her blouse, groaning when the buttons popped open. Dipping my head, I sucked a nipple straight through the silk of her bra, savoring her sharp cry. She curled her legs around my hips and rocked against the hard ridge of my arousal.

"Dawson." She gasped when I pinched her other nipple.

"Too much?" I asked as I lifted my head, my words coming out ragged.

Her head rolled back and forth against the wall. "Not enough. I need you inside me. *Now.*"

"I can manage that."

I eased her down, and she shimmied out of her jeans. I flicked my fly open, stroking my cock because my release was already threatening. I didn't give her much time, certainly not enough time to get out of her panties.

Lifting her against me roughly, I heard the sound of fabric tearing as I shoved the thin strip of silk out of the way. She seemed to sense I was bordering on desperation, pressing hot, wet kisses on my neck and murmuring words.

With her legs curled around me, I dragged the head of my cock through her slick wetness. "Oh God," I muttered as she rocked in to me, and I sank into her hot, clenching, silky core.

When I was buried to the hilt inside Evie, everything else fell away. The universe narrowed to nothing but us. I held still for a beat, adjusting her in my arms and flicking the clasp between her breasts. Somehow, my shirt had been thrown off in the tangled mess. I wanted to feel her skin against mine. She let out a little satisfied hum when her breasts brushed against my chest.

While it was a hot, rushed joining, the undercurrent of emotion and intimacy struck me fiercely. My heart felt split wide open with a sense of vulnerability. Because if Evie didn't feel *this*, the way I did, I didn't know what I would do.

"Look at me," I murmured, my lips a whisper away from her mouth as my forehead fell to press against hers.

Her deep blue gaze met mine. Only then did I let myself slide back, shifting my hips as I buried myself in her again. We rocked together with little surges as I held her tight against me. The fusion of our joining was slick, and I could feel the ripples wracking her body.

"Dawson ..." Her voice was raw, the sound spinning silk around my heart and cinching tighter and tighter.

She cried out roughly, her pussy squeezing my cock as her head fell back against the wall. After two more deep strokes, my release slammed through me, hitting my body so hard and fast my knees almost buckled. My head fell to her neck, my mouth hot and open against her salty skin as I breathed her in.

We stayed like that, pressed against the wall, for several long moments. I finally gathered myself together enough to lift my head. Her eyes met mine, hazy and unfocused.

Slowly easing her down, I pulled out reluctantly. That's how bad I had it for her. I hated losing the closeness I felt when we were skin to skin and joined together like that. Emotion tossed me asunder—like a piece of driftwood in the ocean simply floating along wherever the current carried me with no way to stop it.

The current, in this case, being Evie herself and the fact I was falling in love with her. She placed her palm on my chest, her touch light against my damp skin.

"Well, I'm going to need another dinner," I said. Hell if I know how I managed to tease, but habits do die hard.

Evie smiled softly. "We never did get dessert."

I grinned, quickly buttoning my jeans while she gathered her clothes. "Shall we order room service then?"

That was how I found myself sharing an ice cream sundae with Evie on the bed in our hotel.

The following morning, we met Chad for breakfast at Candy's old diner. She'd sold it when she returned to her hometown, and the new owners had renamed it Dana's Diner.

Dana had waited tables here back when Candy owned it, so I knew her. She was warm and soft with her gray hair tied up in a bun, and a wide smile graced her face the moment she saw me.

"Well, isn't it good to see you here, Dawson?" She squeezed my shoulder as she stopped by our table. "You boys want to start with coffee?"

At our nods, she looked at Evie. "And how about you, dear?"

"I'll take a coffee too," Evie replied.

After Dana left to get our coffees, we flipped through the menu. When Dana returned, we quickly ordered, and it didn't escape me that Dana cast an assessing look at Evie. "You know, Dawson's never brought a girl home. So I'm guessing you two are serious," she commented as she tucked her pencil behind her ear.

Evie's cheeks bloomed pink. Rather than letting her fumble through it, I slid an arm around her shoulders. "Now, Dana, don't scare her off."

Dana chuckled. "It's nice to see you. I hope you get a chance to see your mama."

"Already have."

My uncle Joe's voice interrupted us. "Well, well," Joe said as he approached the table.

Tension coiled in my gut. Joe was my father's only

brother, and let's just say they weren't all that different. Dana's eyes slid sideways, her gaze sobering. Joe was an asshole and well known for being one around town.

"Hey, Uncle Joe," Chad said, his tone calm, but I could sense his underlying tension.

Dana nodded in Joe's direction. "I'll take care of these orders," she said before hurrying off.

Downright relieved this small table only had three chairs, I had less than zero interest in my uncle joining us. Joe's once blond hair was now all gray and thinning. Stopping by Chad's chair, he shifted his eyes to Evie. I wanted to tell him to just leave.

"Didn't know you were coming to town," he said, pulling out the toothpick that was perpetually in his mouth.

"You know I come every few months for a visit. How've you been?"

"Fine. So the old house is on the market?" he asked.

"Ah, should've known there was a reason you were stopping by," I said, not even bothering to hide my frustration. Just like my dad, everything was about weighing the costs and benefits with Joe. He wouldn't go out of his way to greet me for the sake of saying hi. It was all a transaction for him.

Joe's gaze went flat. "Fuck you, Dawson. You're not even around town. I don't know why you gotta say that shit."

"Look," my brother interjected, "that house belonged to our grandparents. Dad didn't put a penny into it."

Joe stared at Chad, and I could sense his mind spinning, trying to find an angle. He was always looking for an easy opportunity to make money.

"His name isn't on it?"

I shook my head slowly. "Dude, you are fucking something else. You know damn well our mother inherited that house from her parents. They had enough sense to write the deed so she couldn't transfer it to anyone but us."

Joe's eyes swung to me again. "Oh, fuck off. You're the

most like your dad of the whole bunch. Always moody and shit when you were a kid."

Chad stood. "Joe ..." he warned.

Joe rolled his eyes and blessedly turned to leave. My brother followed him out. My guess was Chad intended to tell him to stay the fuck away from me. Joe and I had almost come to blows one day after my father's death. He's the one who sold my dad the drugs that killed him.

With a sigh, I looked at Evie. Her hands were tight around her coffee mug. When she met my eyes, hers flashed with anger. "Well, he's an asshole."

"I'm sorry you had to see that."

"Don't apologize, Dawson. I'm just sorry you have to deal with things like that." She paused, her eyes searching mine. "Don't listen to him."

"What are you talking about?"

"Him saying you're like your dad. He's just trying to be an asshole and get to you. It's bullshit. I might not have known your father, but you're a good man. Don't let anyone tell you otherwise."

My heart squeezed in my chest. Evie, with nothing but kindness to scatter about, felt protective of me. I couldn't help myself when I leaned over and pressed a kiss to her temple and then slid my hand around the nape of her neck and caught her lips with mine.

I meant for it to be a brief kiss. But, as was always the case, the moment her sweet lips were on mine, I wanted more. I couldn't help but swipe my tongue across the seam of her lips. That little catch in the back of her throat clenched at my heart like a fist. When I drew back, her cheeks were nice and pink. I loved it. By just being herself, Evie had dissipated the cloud Joe left behind. I could take care of myself, but with Evie here, everything felt better.

Dana arrived with our food, sliding our plates on the table quickly before racing to the next table.

"He's right, you know?"

"About what?" Evie asked as she spread her napkin over her lap.

"I was a moody boy."

She shrugged lightly. "So what? You also had a father who was violent to you and your mother. I don't see why you wouldn't be moody," she said so matter-of-factly I didn't even know what to do with it.

Chad returned to the table, effectively ending our conversation as I struggled to gain my footing internally.

Chapter Seventeen

EVIE

A full two weeks had passed since I went to the coast with Dawson. Autumn had taken hold in the mountains, banishing the lingering heat of summer. The nights were chilly, and the days were getting cooler. The almost oppressive edge of the summer heat was long gone.

Dawson had been busy, and so had I. While he worked from dawn until dusk between guiding hikes, construction on the new cabins, and his work for the first responder crew, I stayed busy in the restaurant. No matter how crazy our days were, we spent most of our nights together unless he had an overnight camping trip.

He was due back from three nights away late this afternoon, and I couldn't wait to see him. I kept telling myself I needed to get a grip. My wishful thinking around him was rampaging out of control. Although we never spoke of it, I was starting to get uncomfortable with the amorphous quality of our relationship. I didn't even know if I could call it a relationship.

I had fallen for Dawson, and I didn't know what the hell to do about it. When we were together, everything just felt *right*. When we were intimate—and there was plenty of that because I could *not* get enough of him—I sensed he felt the way I did. But outside of that, I didn't know. We were still trying to keep things somewhat private. He rarely showed affection in front of anyone we worked with, but then I didn't either.

Yet here and there, I sensed a kernel of distance planted inside him. I also had my own sense of self-preservation. I still couldn't believe Dawson liked me. *Me!*

I was Evie Blair, the shy girl in high school who wanted to hide from the world because her twin sister had died and didn't know how to recover from that grief. When you're a twin, you learn that only other twins really understand. Krista and I had been inseparable before she died. After a few hard years of being awkward with a little bullying sprinkled in and dealing with what felt like insurmountable grief, it had done a number on me.

Those ghosts made it hard for me to believe what Dawson saw in me could be something real. No matter how *real* it felt when we were together.

Walking out of the staff kitchen late that afternoon, Gloria meandered up to me. The giant pig paused in front of me, nudging her nose against my knees. Most of the animals stayed over at the rescue portion of the lodge, but Gloria was friendly and mellow, so she wandered about freely. "Hey, Gloria," I murmured, leaning over to scratch lightly between her ears. With a satisfied snuffle, she gave me a last nudge and kept on walking.

Seeing as all paths in my mind led back to Dawson, I recalled seeing him kneeling on the ground in the rescue barn one afternoon. He'd been feeding snacks to Gloria and Squeaky—Squeaky being the aptly named mini-pig who squeaked quite often. Dawson was patient and kind with animals and often helped Jackson in the rescue when he needed a hand. Only now, it occurred to me I should have known there was more depth to him just because of his kindness to animals.

I realized I'd been standing there mentally drifting off when I heard a car door slam in the guest parking lot. With a start, I strode quickly away.

That night, Dawson showed up at my cabin. At the sound of his knock, I opened the door a crack and looked out to see him. When his silver-gray eyes crinkled at the corners with one of his smiles, my heart did a little victory dance, and my belly spun in flips.

"Hey stranger," I said, swinging the door open.

"Hey," he replied. Leaning against the inside of the doorframe on his shoulder, he looked relaxed and a bit tired.

"You just dropping by to say hey?" I teased.

"Already said that. I was hoping you might let me in for a lot more than a few minutes."

I giggled as he stepped through the door, dropped his bag to the floor, and swept me into his arms. I loved how easily he held me and the feel of his hard, muscled body against mine.

"Oh, sweetheart," he murmured into my hair.

The cool autumn air blew in with him as he kicked the door shut with his boot and spun me around, pressing me to the door and kissing me senseless.

"How was your trip?" I asked a few moments later when we finally had to come up for air.

"Good. I love the hikes. I might've missed you, though," he said, his gaze sliding sideways as if gauging how I was going to react.

Even though it scared me a little, I decided to be honest. "I definitely missed you."

His slow smile was enough to melt me as he leaned over to kiss me again. "Okay," he said when we came up for air again, "I definitely missed you. And I'm fucking starving."

"I planned ahead," I said as I shimmied out from between him and the door.

I hurried over to the small kitchenette in the corner and pulled out the still warm pizza Dani had made for us.

"Oh, girl," Dawson said as I turned with the pizza box in hand. "You're gonna kill me."

We nibbled on pizza and flicked through channels on the television before he fell asleep propped up against the pillows, his exhaustion getting the best of him. I quietly put the pizza away, sliding the small box into the mini fridge before pulling his boots off. He didn't even wake as I did that. When I pulled his jeans off, he barely moved but woke briefly.

"Oh, sorry, Evie," he slurred. "Didn't mean to fall asleep on you."

I gave his jeans a good tug to get them free from his ankles. He was so tired he wasn't much help. "No need to apologize," I murmured as I rounded the bed and brushed his hair away from his eyes before dusting a kiss on his lips.

Of course, the sight of him in his fitted black briefs had the usual effects on my insides, but he needed sleep. I tugged the covers from underneath and tucked them over him. In another second, his breathing had fallen back into the steady, even breath of sleep.

Hours later in the darkness, I felt Dawson's hands mapping my body. "Mmm, you feel so good," he murmured against my neck.

"Dawson," I gasped, my voice a ragged whisper.

He slid inside me from behind, bringing me to an achingly piercing climax in a matter of seconds. I loved the feel of him shuddering against me as his hot release filled me. As we lay there, his phone began to buzz insistently from where he'd left it on the night table.

When he didn't move, I finally nudged him with my elbow. "Dawson, Dawson?"

"Mmm-hmm?"

"Your phone keeps buzzing. I think someone needs you. Are you on call?"

He sat up abruptly, and I instantly missed him wrapped around me and buried inside. Rubbing his eyes, he gave his head a shake.

"Huh? No, I'm never on call right when I get back from a trip." He fumbled for his phone, answering, "Dawson."

I heard the indecipherable reply on the other end and felt his body tighten immediately. "She okay?"

A long pause followed when I could hear nothing more than the subtle murmurs on the other end.

"Okay. I'll leave within a half hour. I'll see you by early afternoon," he said to whoever was on the line.

By this point, I was wide-awake. I slid up, propping the pillows behind me against the headboard. "Is everything okay?" I asked as he set the phone down, swinging his feet off the side of the bed.

"My mom's in the hospital. I gotta get going."

"Oh, no! What happened?" I asked, kicking the covers back.

He stood, looking over at me, his face tight. The night-light from the corner cast a soft glow across his face. "My brother said she had one of her coughing fits and passed out. With her emphysema and congestive heart failure, they thought it best to hospitalize her. The hospital called him. I need to shower and go."

Before I had a chance to reply, he turned and strode into the bathroom. "Do you mind if I shower here?" he called over his shoulder.

"Of course not." I climbed out of bed, intending to make some coffee. Glancing at the clock, I saw that it was only four thirty in the morning. Dani wouldn't be up yet, so there would be no coffee over at the lodge kitchen for him to grab.

As I prepped the coffee and listened to the water running in the bathroom, I wondered what to do. I wanted to offer to go with him, but I didn't know if he wanted me to, nor if I could. I had double shifts for the next few days since one of our regulars was out of town and another had a nasty cold.

I snagged my robe off the hook on the bathroom door and shrugged into it. Just as I was considering whether to ask Dawson about going with him, he came out, rubbing his hair with a towel. I had turned the lamp on beside the bed, and his eyes flicked from there to the coffee. “You’re the best, Evie.”

“Want company?”

My question decided to ask itself. I almost slapped my hand over my mouth when it slipped out.

Dawson stood there, staring at me blankly for a moment. “Don’t get me wrong, I’d love for you to go, but I know you’re booked up. I ran into Dani when I was walking by the lodge last night. You work, I’ll go check on my mom, and I’ll be back.”

I took a breath and let it out slowly. “Your mother will be fine.”

Dawson turned away, stepping over to the bag he brought in with him last night. He tugged out a clean pair of jeans and a T-shirt as he replied, “I hope so. She’s had bouts like this before, and her doctor tells us we should expect it.”

When he turned back, I could see the uncertainty in his eyes, and I wanted to hug him and tell him it would be okay, but I didn’t. Instead, with uncertainty hanging in the air between us, I turned and poured him a cup of coffee.

My heart felt funny, and my throat felt tight. I was in love with Dawson Marsh, and I needed to figure out what to do about it.

When I turned back, my breath was knocked clean from my lungs. Dawson with damp hair from a shower and a pair of jeans without a shirt on was a sight almost too yummy. Although we’d been doing this dance for over a month now, I had yet to get accustomed to seeing him. He was so delicious, need shot through me just looking at him.

Willfully pushing those feelings away, I reached for the

travel mug. "To-go cup," I said, holding it out. "You'll text me when you get there?"

"Absolutely."

"And you'll let me know how she is?"

Stepping close, I placed my palm on his chest over his heart, feeling it thud against his ribs and my own lunging in response.

"Of course, I will."

"If you need me, just say so."

Dawson took another step, taking the coffee from me and brushing my hair back from my forehead. A little shiver chased in the wake of his touch where his fingers brushed along the side of my neck as he tucked my hair behind my ear. "You're too good to me, Evie."

He punctuated his words with kisses. One on my temple and another on my cheek as he captured my chin in his hand lightly. His kiss was gentle, just a brush of his lips across mine, yet when he lifted his head, I was on fire, and my heart was pounding so hard it wouldn't have surprised me if he heard it.

"I hope I'll be back in a few days. I'll text you as soon as I get there."

With that, he was gone, the chilly morning air gusting through the door as he stepped through. Without thinking, I followed him, standing on the porch and watching as he walked into the darkness. It wasn't even dawn yet.

Chapter Eighteen

EVIE

Dawson: I'm here. My mom's going to be OK.

I stared at Dawson's text, smiling slowly. He wasn't too wordy when he texted. Funny as he was, his humor didn't usually come across via text. He was typically straight and to the point.

Me: I'm so glad. Give her my best. When will she be out of the hospital?

Dawson: Probably tomorrow morning. Just a scare. They want to keep her for the night to monitor her and make sure she's stable. Her doctor made some adjustments to her medications.

I wanted to ask how long he planned to stay, but that felt selfish. I opted for two emoticons—a smile and a thankful symbol.

Dawson: I should be back the day after tomorrow. My brother's got something going on with the house sale. Might as well stay so I can sign whatever he needs me to.

As if he'd intuited my question, he answered it. Knowing Dawson's reaction when his brother brought up the house sale before, I worried about how he was doing. But I wasn't going to try to have a conversation like that via text.

Me: OK. I hope it goes smoothly.

Dawson: Oh, it will. If we don't close on the sale, I'll use that opportunity to sign my portion over to my brother.

I smiled a little. Dawson wasn't a greedy person. The more I learned about him, the deeper I fell. He'd let it casually slip once that he used every extra bit of money he had to cover his mother's long-term care insurance. He was a good man and a loving son.

I wasn't thinking too hard when I replied.

Me: I'll miss you until you get back. Text me tomorrow to let me know how things are going?

Dawson: You got it. Miss you.

I didn't realize that I'd practically been leaning forward inside, hoping he would tell me he missed me.

"What's that smile for?" Grace asked as she leaned against the shelves beside me in the pantry.

I'd gotten marooned in here just coming to get a few things. "Oh, Dawson texted me and said he missed me," I replied.

I didn't even care to try to play it cool. I practically wanted to do cartwheels and shout it to the world.

Grace smiled. "You've got it bad, girl. I'd be worried about you if it wasn't so obvious Dawson's got it bad too."

"Didn't you come back here to get some things for the line cooks?" she asked with a giggle.

"Oh, right, I did." Slipping my phone back in my purse hanging on a hook on the wall, I quickly scanned the shelves. "I might need some man advice."

Grace's gaze slid to mine as she helped me pull jars of olives and red peppers off the shelf and stack them on a tray. "What man advice do you need?"

"Man advice?" Dani's voice carried through the pantry door.

We turned back in unison. "My fault I'm behind. I got hung up," I offered.

"How about you two finish this shift, and we'll schedule

man advice after that? You're both done in an hour, same as me. Let's have a bottle of wine, and I am *all* over the man advice. But right now, we just had four new tables come in."

Hours later, after the restaurant was closed for the night, I sat on a stool by the large stainless-steel table in the private portion of the kitchen where Dani often worked on special projects and cooked for the staff.

"Red or white?" Grace called from where she stood in front of the wine rack.

"Red," I called in return.

"White," Dani replied at the same time.

Dani was jotting something in a notepad and glanced up with a smile. "There're four of us. We can finish two bottles. If not, we'll save the rest for later this week."

Dani had the foresight to toss a pizza in the oven while the dinner shift wound down. Seeing as I had forgotten to eat, I was relieved. Of course, when Dani threw together some pizza, it was flat-out gourmet. Her homemade crust and sauce were divine. This one was half pepperoni with red sauce and half with a buttered crust and fresh basil, garlic, olives, and feta.

I slid another pepperoni piece off the plate in the center of the table and took a bite. After I finished chewing, I sighed. "Oh my God. This is so good."

Valentina came in from the back hallway, sitting down across from me and smiling as she reached up to tighten her ponytail. "I'm so freaking hungry," she said as she reached over and helped herself to two slices.

Dani flashed a small smile as she helped herself to a slice of the basil and garlic. "Most of us forgot to eat tonight."

Grace slipped her hips onto the stool beside Dani, handing her the bottle of white wine. "Already opened them," she said, gesturing to the wineglasses on the table.

Within a few minutes, we had all had a piece of pizza and were sipping on our choice of wine.

"Okay, who needed man advice?" Dani asked.

Grace pointed at me as she finished chewing a bite of pizza.

"Oh, that's right. You and Dawson. How are things?" Valentina said with a grin.

"Dawson told Evie he misses her," Grace offered before taking a sip of her wine.

I felt my cheeks heat and ignored it. "That's what he texted."

"Well, do you miss him?" Valentina asked.

"Yes. He went to see his mother. It sounds like she's going to be okay, but I wish I'd gone with him."

"Why didn't you?" Dani asked as she reached for another slice of pizza, pausing to snag a napkin from the stack in the center of the table.

"I thought about offering to go, but I didn't feel right about leaving you in the lurch for shifts."

Dani took a bite, shaking her head as she did. After she finished chewing, she canted her head to the side. "I appreciate your responsibility, but you could've asked. I mean, if it's for love, we could've figured something out," she said with a grin.

"I'd offered to cover, but I was already on duty this weekend, so it wouldn't help," Grace commented.

"I know you would," I said, flashing her a smile.

"So what man advice do you need?" Valentina asked.

Valentina exuded a strange combination of innocent and wise. Although Lucas was her first everything, and their relationship was still fresh, she had a much better grasp on relationships than most of us. I suppose it was because she didn't hide what she felt. It also helped that Lucas was utterly and totally in love with her.

"I don't know. This thing with Dawson, well, it kind of came out of nowhere."

"Nowhere?" Dani asked, her brows hitching up so high they almost disappeared into her hairline. "You two have been dancing around each other ever since he started working here."

I waved a hand dismissively. "Dawson is a flirt. That's just how he is."

"Oh, we know that," Grace piped up, "but the way he flirts with you has always been different from the way he flirts in general. You're special."

"What does that mean?"

Valentina brushed one of her red curls out of her eyes and smiled at me. "Just that. It's always been obvious that he likes you. He teases most guys as much as women. With you, it's a *thing*."

"Okay, fine. So the general consensus is this thing with Dawson didn't come out of nowhere. But I don't know what we are."

"What do you mean?" Grace countered, pausing to finish her slice of pizza as she waited for me to answer.

"I don't know how to define us. Are we like dating-dating? I mean, he says he misses me, and I'll admit that's kind of awesome, but I can't let myself read too much into this."

"What do you want?" Valentina asked, getting right to the point as she was wont to do.

My stomach felt funny, and my heart started thudding hard in my chest as clarity slammed into me. I'd gone and fallen in love—totally and completely. The more I got to know Dawson, the harder it was to keep my feelings at bay.

Taking a breath, I masked my sudden emotional distress with a few sips of wine. As if my friends could sense what was up, they all stayed quiet. No one pushed me. They just let me sit with whatever I was muddling through.

"I guess I want something serious," I finally said.

"That's what I thought." Valentina's gaze held mine, clear

blue with soft understanding and empathy shining back at me. "I recognize the signs," she said with a small smile.

"Oh, God, what am I going to do?" I wailed, putting my face in my hands. "I have no idea what he wants."

"Okay, let's rewind," Dani interjected, all business as usual. Dani was a problem solver if there ever was one. "So you guys have hot sex because you can't help it. Have you ever talked about what's happening? Or is it just happening?"

"Not much," I said, finally lifting my head and brushing my hair away from my face. "When it all started, I told Dawson I wasn't so sure it was a good idea, and he said that we should take it one step at a time. I'm just worried. I don't have a lot of experience with serious relationships, like hardly any, and as far as I can tell, he has none, like zero."

"Maybe you should start by telling him how you feel," Valentina offered.

I looked over at her and sighed. "Easy for you to say. Lucas is so in love with you, it's amazing he doesn't trip and fall every time he sees you."

Valentina's cheeks pinkened, and she rolled her eyes. "It wasn't always obvious. I'm just saying the only way to get clarity is to try to talk about it. That's all."

Grace caught my eyes and wrinkled her nose. "It's true. I've only had one serious relationship—which totally blew up in my face—but you have to try to talk when you're not sure."

"They say most communication is nonverbal, so let's look at what Dawson's nonverbal communication tells us," Dani interjected.

"Well, as far as I can tell, the sex is awesome," Grace offered. "I mean, if we're going on how he gives you those hot looks all the time."

"Oh yeah, we've all seen how he looks at you," Valentina interjected with an arch of her brow.

I burst out laughing. "But what about the baggage? There's always baggage. I mean, I have baggage. I can't believe a man who looks like Dawson wants me. You know what high school was like for me," I said, looking at Grace. Because we'd known each other for so long and were the same age, Grace knew how brutal high school had been for me.

"Of course we all have baggage, but you are *totally* hot. No matter what you think in your head, Dawson likes you. Whether it has anything to do with your looks isn't really the point," Valentina offered. "He's got plenty of beautiful women to pick from if that's all it's about."

Chapter Nineteen

DAWSON

Curling my hands around the wheelchair handles, I rolled my mother through the door into the assisted living home.

"You didn't have to come," she said, glancing up to look at me over her shoulder.

"Mom, when you end up at the hospital, you can expect me to show up. No need to argue about it after the fact."

The receptionist waved to us, and my mother threw a smile her way as I turned down the hallway that led to my mother's room. A few minutes later, she was situated in her favorite chair by the windows with the new e-book reader I'd gotten for her a few months ago, along with her favorite lemon and honey tea.

I sank into the chair at an angle across from her, leaning back with a sigh. I hadn't wanted to bother with a hotel room, so I had some semblance of sleep in the chairs at the hospital last night.

My mother took a sip of her tea and cocked her head to the side. "So I liked meeting Evie," she said, her tone casual as if she were discussing the weather.

Nothing was ever casual with my mother, and I damn

well knew it. I grinned. "I'm amazed it took you this long to mention her."

My mother rolled her eyes and laughed softly. "She means something to you. I can tell."

She didn't even ask how I felt. My mother was like that. She didn't tiptoe around issues. Maybe it was because she'd been through so much. Her willingness to tolerate any bullshit ended years ago, and she called things how she saw them.

Sometimes that was comforting, and sometimes it was unsettling. Just now, I rolled my shoulders, wishing my feelings for Evie weren't so blatantly obvious. Because hell if I knew how to navigate this.

"She does," I finally said.

My mother was quiet for a minute, looking out the window beside her with the ocean in the distance through the trees. When she looked back toward me, her gaze was contemplative. "You know, I still worry about you."

"Because of Dad?"

We'd had our conversations about him. Many times. This was a topic better left alone as far as I was concerned.

"Not in the way you think," she replied.

"What do you mean then?"

"None of this makes what your father did okay. He used alcohol, and then pills, and often violence to handle the way he felt inside. It was a terrible choice, one that hurt everyone who mattered to him. I won't even bother to say he loved any of us. He was too far gone to register that level of emotion. My point is, though, when I first knew him, he wasn't like that. When he was young, he struggled with depression sometimes like you do."

My gut churned, and I swallowed. I didn't want to have this conversation. "Mom, don't fucking tell me I'm like him," I said, my voice holding a sharp edge.

"Honey, you're nothing like your father. You have a heart of gold, you protected me, and you protected your brother when you were way too young to have ever had to worry about that. I completely understand why you want nothing to do with the house. I just figured you should be the one to get the money and not me. Because I don't need it. I'm not going to live much longer."

I opened my mouth to argue, but my mother held up her hand. "Honey, don't. I'm sick. I'm doing okay, but I definitely won't be here for much longer. For all you did to try to keep the rest of us safe, I figured you might as well get the money. If you choose to give it to your brother, fine. But I'd like it to be your decision, not mine. That's not what I want to talk about. I just wanted to say that there is one thing you do share with your dad and with me. I know you get depressed sometimes. I saw it when you were a teenager. Back then, you had so much to do to take care of your brother and me. In a way, it was what held you together. That and your sense of humor." She paused, smiling softly. "You are so funny, and you always were. You became such a tease and flirt when you got older. Over the past few years, I worried about that because that was how you kept everyone at a little bit of a distance. When I saw you with Evie, that was the first time in a long time I saw you just being *you* without the need for the rest."

I took a deep breath, letting it out slowly. "And what? What's your point?"

"I'm glad to see you're letting yourself be who you are. Having watched your father run from his demons, I see what that can do to a person. Don't think for a second, not even a millisecond, that I would ever worry you would make choices the way your father did. I just mean that it's okay to let yourself sit with things. Trust me, I know what it's like to want to escape. I wouldn't want you to be alone. You always were a sweet boy, and I know you'll make an amazing partner for someone."

It felt as if tiny balls were bouncing around in my mind, the sound a cacophony. A sense of panic was blasting me, but

I didn't want to face it. I heard everything my mother said, and I understood it logically and intellectually, but there was a good reason I never wanted anyone to matter too much to me. I truly didn't worry about becoming like my father. Violence had never been an option for me, and it didn't seem I was susceptible to his problems with substances. Oh sure, I drank, but it never got out of control. In a way, I almost had to push that envelope to test it.

Yet here and there, those times when that heavy feeling of darkness weighed on me, my escape hatch wasn't working anymore. I didn't know what the hell to do with Evie. My mother had gone quiet again, leaving me to mentally flail about on my own.

I managed to scramble myself together inside, but that sense of panic was still buzzing under the surface.

"It's okay to care about somebody." My mother's voice sounded as if it were far away.

I turned to find her warm blue eyes waiting. Once upon a time, all I'd see in her gaze was weariness and fear. That was long gone, and the wisdom that came in its wake was sometimes too painful to tolerate, especially when directed at me.

"I know it is, Mom. Evie and I are pretty fresh, so—"

My words trailed off with a shrug, and my mother smiled softly. "I gathered that. I like her, and it's pretty obvious you mean something to her."

Blessedly, my brother showed up then. We had an offer on the house, and we intended to take it. After I said goodbye to my mother, we went to the realtor's office. Chad had made sure the friendly realtor, Karen, had all the paperwork set up ahead of time. He knew this situation was a sore spot for me and that I simply wanted the house gone because it held too many bad memories for me. The only good memories were points of respite between the madness. It wasn't as if my father knocked us around every day, yet during the in-between times, we were all waiting for the next explosion.

"So I just need both of you to sign here," the realtor said. "I'll have you know, your uncle tried to make a claim on the deed." Her eyes flicked to my brother. "Thanks for the heads-up. I had all the paperwork showing the transfer of the property from your mother's parents to her."

I rolled my eyes. For a moment, I waited for the rise of anger inside, but a sense of relief came instead. "Thank you," I said, looking back and forth between them.

Karen looked from Chad to me. "Onto the next slightly awkward topic. When you called and said you wanted everything signed over to your brother, I prepared all the paperwork for that. But he was one step ahead of you and had already set up a trust, directing that the money be set aside for you if you should ever choose to access it." Karen's eyes bounced between us as if prepared for some kind of argument.

I started laughing. "Dude, you are not gonna let me just give this to you, are you?"

Chad laughed, but his gaze sobered quickly. "No. If it weren't for you, my life would be very different right now. You've paid all Mom's bills, and you put me through college at a time when I don't think you could really afford it. Maybe this'll mean you can get your own house. Mom's parents owned a huge chunk of property, a lot more than we knew. She hid it from Dad and never even mentioned it to me. Half of it is more than enough for you to set yourself up and buy a place clean and clear, just like I can. Don't even try to argue because I'm ready for you."

My throat got tight. Leaning back, I stared at the ceiling for a moment as I gathered myself. Leveling my gaze with his again, I said, "Fine. You're right anyway. It's not really Dad's place. It was always Mom's, to begin with."

Although I left town later that afternoon feeling better than I had in years, one thing still weighed on me. I didn't know what the hell to do about Evie and how much I missed her.

Two days. Two fucking days, and I missed her so much, my heart viscerally ached. I had no idea how to do this. I knew how to take care of myself and my family, but I didn't know how to do love. Darkness had laid claim to my father. It was something that terrified me because I knew that urge to escape, to flee the feeling. I didn't think I would ever die of a drug overdose. One therapist I'd seen when I was younger—all but forced to go to by a social worker investigating my parents—had shared that people who experienced abuse didn't always follow in the footsteps of those who doled it out. Sometimes, they learned the behavior without awareness and repeated it, or they had a reaction against it.

My reaction against it was so strong it almost hurt. I eschewed all violence. But I could control that. I couldn't control the dark days. My brother struggled with those days as well because I recognized it in him. Sometimes it came out of nowhere, sneaking in when you least expected it. Like a sunny day when the clouds drifted in and blocked the light or a thunderstorm rolling in so quickly it obliterated the brightness in a matter of minutes.

I didn't know how to do a relationship, and Evie had come to mean so much to me. I wanted to get it right for her, but I had no clue how to do that.

I tried to tell myself I shouldn't go straight to see her when I got back to Stolen Hearts Lodge. But it was as if my feet had a mind of their own. They walked straight to her cabin even though it was past midnight. My knuckles rapped lightly on her door, expecting her to be asleep and not answer.

Instead, the door swung open. Evie stood there in her robe with her cheeks a little pink, and her hair tousled around her shoulders. Before I could think, I was stepping through the door, cupping her face with my hands, and kissing her as if my life depended on it.

Evie murmured my name just before my mouth claimed hers. If she was surprised at my intensity, it didn't show. She melted into it. Her mouth opened under mine with a low moan.

I poured everything into our kiss—my confusion, my uncertainty, my wish to be a man I wasn't, and to have faith in myself on this shaky ground. Tangled within all that was the shining certainty of one thing—against all odds, I had fallen in love with Evie.

Chapter Twenty

DAWSON

Sometime later, after I had taken Evie roughly, we lay panting on her bed. I felt as if I had been washed ashore after a storm, after being battered by the wind and the waves. The force of our joining was so powerful it ruined me.

As the thunder of my heartbeat gradually slowed, I felt Evie's fingers trail over my arm. "Well, I missed you," she said with a low laugh.

Rolling my head to the side, I let myself soak in the sight of her. Her dark hair was spread in a tangle on the pillow. She rolled on her side, her cheeks flushed pink and her skin dewy.

"I missed you too." The words felt strange when I said them aloud. I hadn't ever expected to miss someone the way I'd missed her the past few days.

She was so quiet I could hear the beat of my heart in my ears, and the weight of my emotions frightened me. It was unfamiliar and disconcerting. I managed to take a breath, but it wasn't easy.

"So your mom is okay?" she asked softly.

Swallowing, I nodded. "She is."

It said something that this topic felt like safe territory emotionally. Despite the mess of my childhood, I'd always had a tight bond with my mother, and I didn't shy away from it. Since she'd been sick for years now, I'd also become accustomed to the reality of what that meant. I recalled something she had said years back. Her own mother had lingered after having cancer, and my mother had helped to care for her. She'd once told me it was like saying goodbye a piece at a time. She had wondered if it was easier to let go all at once, rather than in increments.

In the end, it didn't matter. Life dealt you the hand of cards, and you had no choice but to play them as best you could.

Evie seemed to sense I didn't want to talk much and let the quiet envelop us. I surmised she thought it was because I didn't want to talk about my mother. That wasn't it.

The persistent buzzing of my emergency cell nudged me out of sleep. I didn't want to leave Evie's warmth and softness—most specifically, her.

It didn't matter, though. Her eyes opened as I rose slowly, trying to carefully untangle myself from her. "What is it?" she asked, her voice husky from sleep like crushed velvet.

I pressed a kiss to her cheek. "I've got a call. Need to go."

Jackson had offered to switch up the schedule since I'd taken the past two days to visit my mother, but I'd texted and told him there was no need. I stood quickly, tugging on my clothes and leaving. Walking out into the chilly autumn dawn, I beat back the slight sense of panic churning in my gut. Back when I'd done my training to become a first responder, my current chief had told me I was rock solid in a crisis.

The one and only call that had shaken me—that fucking

overdose that looked too damn much like my own father's death—hadn't shaken me at the moment, only later. In a strange way, I found solace in being able to stay calm in a crisis. When your whole childhood felt out of control, there was something powerful about being able to manage situations for other people.

But with Evie, I felt completely out of control. I'd come back last night, desperate to see her, only to find the sense of solace shattered. Because I didn't have a way to contain my feelings for her. I had no way to keep them in check.

That morning—working with Lucas, Jackson, and Wade as we dealt with a nasty car accident—I concluded there was only one way to manage it, and that was to stop it.

I ignored the part of my heart that wanted to throw a fucking tantrum over it. I figured I had already faced enough of my demons in this life. For years, I found a way to keep my internal peace. I just needed to find my way back to that.

Chapter Twenty-One

EVIE

"Ow!" I released the handle of the skillet, shaking my hand rapidly and spinning around to dash to the closest sink.

The icy water eased the sting of the burn.

"You okay?" Dani asked from over my shoulder.

Brushing my hair away from my face with the back of my wrist, I glanced over at her. "Yeah, I'm fine. Should've used a potholder."

"What the hell are you doing in the kitchen, anyway?" She leaned her hips against the wide stainless-steel sink, eyeing me as I turned off the water and dried my hands.

"Good question. I thought I'd help get orders ready."

She arched a brow, her perceptive gaze coasting over me. "In the kitchen? That's what we have the line cooks for. Don't take this the wrong way, but I sure as hell don't need you burning your hand trying to be helpful."

I sighed, nodding as I turned to lean my hips against the sink beside her. "Point taken."

Dani glanced at the round clock above the door that led from the kitchen to the restaurant. "Aren't you almost done, anyway?"

"I volunteered to cover for Grace tonight. She has a migraine."

Dani nodded. "I wish she'd go to the doctor. Is it just me, or is she getting those more often?"

"It's not just you. I told her last week she should talk to her doctor about it. She didn't want to listen."

Dani shook her head before replying to something one of the line cooks said. She turned back and added, "And please keep Evie out of the kitchen."

Paul chuckled, throwing a wink my way. "Yes, ma'am. I didn't ask her to help."

"I know you didn't." Dani looked back at me. "How about some coffee with me out back before the dinner rush hits?" she asked, nudging her chin toward the door leading into the private portion of the kitchen.

Seeing as I could use the coffee because I hadn't slept well in over a week, I nodded. She simply turned and walked to the back with me.

"Just made this," she said moments later as she slid a cup of coffee in front of me, pushing over a small container of cream.

I added a dash before sliding it back in her direction. After the first sip, I sighed as I leaned back in my chair. She insisted we come all the way into her office where we were seated at a small round table in the corner.

Dani took a long swallow from her coffee before lasering her gaze on me. "What the hell is going on?"

"What do you mean?" I countered, knowing full well she was asking about my not-so-great mood over the past week.

"Hmm, let's see. You're cranky, you're irritable, you look like you're barely sleeping, and as far as I can tell, you and Dawson aren't talking."

I'd hardly seen him. According to Jackson, he offered to be on call every single night since he got back from visiting his mom. Needless to say, between his work here and that, he hadn't really been around for me to see. It hurt. It *really* hurt. Because whether he told me or not—newsflash, he didn't, and it sucked—I knew he was calling it quits on us.

"I guess he's busy," was my lame, evasive reply.

Dani took a slow sip of her coffee, never once taking her eyes away from me. "He's definitely busy. So are you. Now that you mention it, you've picked up four extra shifts this week. Something else is up."

Just thinking about Dawson made my throat hurt and my eyes sting with unshed tears. I didn't really want to talk about him because I didn't know what to say.

I felt like an idiot. Something had shifted that last night we were together. I felt it before he even fell asleep. Being busy wasn't what was going on with him.

I shrugged. "I don't know what's up with him," I offered, my words catching in my throat.

Dani's gaze softened. "Hey, I didn't mean to hit a sore spot. I was honestly worried. You're not usually irritable."

I didn't even realize I was crying until she leaned back in her chair, reaching for a box of tissues on her desk and handing it to me. I snagged a tissue, dabbing at my eyes and blowing my nose.

"I'm so stupid," I muttered

"I may not know what's going on, but you're not allowed to call yourself stupid. It's against the rules."

"What rules?" I asked with a sniffle.

"The girlfriend rules. We're not allowed to bash ourselves."

"Um, okay. Well, I *feel* stupid. Dawson was always out of my league, and I knew it. I'm sure he never meant for this to be anything more than a little fun, and now he's done with the fun. I'm the one who started to read too much into it."

Dani's breath came out in a startled puff, her eyes widening. "You're funny, smart, and totally cute. Plus, looks aren't what matter."

I dabbed at my nose with a balled-up tissue and sighed. "You know what I mean. Dawson's hot."

"Actually, I don't know what you mean. I remember high school, and I know how hard it was for you even if we weren't close then. But you were still cute, and you've been a bit of a flirt ever since college."

I shrugged. "So? It's all just superficial. Fake it till you make it kind of thing. Dawson's always had women chasing after him. He sure as hell never would've noticed me in high school."

Dani's eyes narrowed. "Forget about high school. High school was hell for most everybody. Plus, Dawson looks as miserable as you do this week."

"So what?"

"I don't think it's as simple as him being done having fun with you. That's all. I'm going to talk to him and find out what his deal is."

"Don't you dare!" I narrowed my eyes and shook my head. I loved Dani, and she was a good friend. But I was not at all about her trying to intervene with Dawson. I'd rather let it just fade away and have things go back to the way they used to be.

My heart felt cracked because I would even miss the way we used to tease each other before we let this go anywhere. *Stupid, stupid, stupid.*

Dani's mouth twisted to the side. I could tell she wanted to argue the point. Much as she was prone to stick her nose in everything, she wouldn't if I asked her not to.

"Please don't try to talk to him about me."

"Fine, I won't. I still don't think it's as simple as you think." She opened her mouth to say something else when someone called her name from the kitchen. "You sure you don't want to just call it a night? We can make do without you."

"Oh, God, no! I need to work. The last thing I need is to go back to my cabin and be bored by myself."

With another call for Dani, she reluctantly stood. I guzzled the rest of my coffee and followed her. I was relieved it was a busy night. I really didn't have time to think, and I certainly didn't want to.

Chapter Twenty-Two

EVIE

Several more days passed uneventfully. Now that I was actively avoiding Dawson as much as he appeared to be avoiding me, I hardly saw him, and that was a relief. When I did see him, even from a distance, there was a sharp sting on my heart. It felt as if the crack just couldn't heal; as if my skin had cracked deeply, and I kept tearing it open, again and again. It hurt like hell.

In my efforts to avoid the pain, I filled my time with work. When I had an open morning, I called my mother and asked her to meet me at Wake & Bake Café. I tried to get together with my parents every few weeks. I was nursing an Americano with an extra shot—the bitterness suited to my mood—when my mother came through the door into the café. She hurried over, pulling me into a quick hug. "Hey, dear, so good to see you," she said as she stepped back.

"You too, Mom. Your coffee's already covered," I said.

"Evelyn, that's not necessary," she said with a soft smile, brushing a loose lock of her silver hair away from her glasses.

Only my mother ever called me Evelyn. I hated it when I was little, but I'd grown strangely fond of her habit a few years after my sister died. She'd called both of us by our full names—Evelyn and Kristalyn. It was a poignant reminder of Krista once the grief faded to a tolerable ache.

Smiling, I shrugged as I sat back down at the small table by the windows. "You can take it up with Nancy."

My mother chuckled, rolling her blue eyes—so similar to mine. She hurried off to order, chatting briefly with Nancy before returning to sit with me. After a few minutes of casual catch-up, my mother cocked her head to the side. "Are you okay?"

My chest tightened, and anxiety spun inside. My relationship with my parents was solid, though sometimes tense. After Krista died, they'd gotten hyper-protective. Years past that, I could understand it was how they coped, but it had made it hard to talk about emotional topics.

But one thing I'd tried really hard to do was not let that get in the way. Because loss taught me brutal lessons about never taking anything for granted. So, I took a gulp of coffee followed by a deep breath and met my mother's concerned gaze. "I'm so-so," I finally said.

"So-so? That tells me almost nothing," my mother said with a hint of a smile.

"Okay, okay. It's a guy thing."

My mother sipped her coffee slowly, her gaze considered. "Since you're giving me next to nothing, I'll guess. You like someone, and it's not going well?" At my nod, she continued. "I doubt you want advice from me, but if there's one thing your dad and I got right, it's commitment. There is no perfect in love. Ever. People screw up all the time. Even after they get things spectacularly right sometimes. If it matters, then do something about it. Whatever you do, don't write someone off if they screw up. If it's worth it, most people figure it out."

"Why would you think I'd write someone off?" I asked, knowing by the sting in my heart she'd zeroed in on a genuine possibility.

"Because you have a stubborn streak. So does your brother. It's possible you got that from me," she replied with a teasing smile.

I chewed on the inside of my cheek and rolled my eyes. At that moment, Nancy stopped by our table. "Y'all need anything else?" she asked.

When we both shook our heads, Nancy shifted gears. "And when is Mack coming home?" she asked, referring to my older brother.

My mother beamed. "Soon, I hope."

Nancy beamed in return. "Well, I know y'all will be glad to see him. I sure will." Pausing, she glanced away when someone called her name from the counter. With an apologetic smile, she looked back at us. "Cranky oven today. Apparently, I've got the magic touch. Good to see you both," she said before hurrying away.

My phone buzzed after that with a text from Dani asking me to cover a shift after one of the waiters had to leave early. Looking up at my mother, I said, "I've gotta go..."

I meant to thank her, but emotion rushed through me, startling me with its intensity. This was nothing more than coffee with my mother, but it meant so much, even more so for how mundane it was. No matter what, she was always there. Even when all she did was remind me not to be too stubborn. Whether or not Dawson figured it out wasn't so much the point. I was teetering on shutting him out.

With my words falling short, my mother reached across the table and squeezed my hand. "Don't worry so much, Evelyn. If it's going to work out, it will."

"That's all?"

Sadness flickered in her eyes. Because I knew, and she knew, just how things couldn't work out. Sometimes you lost people, and it was just random bad luck. When things didn't work out, life kept on whether you wanted it to or not.

On the heels of that flash of sadness, my mother smiled, her eyes twinkling. "Yes. But you already know that."

One night when I had worked late yet again, I was returning to my cabin. The ache of missing Dawson had morphed into a dull, throbbing pain. The lights interspersed throughout the trees guided me back to my cabin. I willfully attempted not to even look in the direction of Dawson's cabin, yet my eyes swung in that direction when I heard the leaves rustle.

I recognized his silhouette in the darkness immediately. He was backlit by the light from his porch, and my eyes soaked him in—the clean line of his jaw, the slope of his strong shoulders, and the easy way he moved, grace and strength spun together.

That crack in my heart stung. My throat hurt, and my eyes pricked with unshed tears. Trying to breathe through the emotion, I looked away. Before I took another step, I heard him exclaim. It sounded as if he were in pain.

My feet turned on their own, and I hurried up the path toward him. "Are you okay?"

Silver-gray eyes met mine, glinting just barely in the light cast from the porch. "Copperhead," he muttered, his tone low and pained.

I realized he was cradling his arm, and my eyes flicked to his wrist. Even in limited light, I could see it was already swelling. I forgot about my cracked heart and my wounded pride. "We have to get you to the hospital now."

"Aw, fuck."

Out of habit, he started to reach into his pocket with his right hand and then swore, shaking his wrist free.

"I've got my phone," I said quickly, yanking it out of my purse. "Who should I call?"

"Jackson. It'll be faster for him to drive me," he murmured. "Be careful, I don't know where the snake went."

Tapping Jackson's contact on my phone screen, I waited, glancing around while the phone rang in my ear. Copperheads were abundant in North Carolina. They tended to hide away, but if they felt threatened, they would bite.

Jackson answered. "Jackson here."

"Jackson, it's Evie, and Dawson told me to call you. He got bit by a copperhead."

"Where are you?"

"On the path in front of his cabin." Pausing, I glanced at Dawson. "Can you walk?"

His features were taut as he nodded. "Of course, I can walk."

Jackson must have heard his reply. "Meet me at the lodge. Go to the back."

"Okay. We'll be there in a few." Ending the call, I stepped closer to Dawson. "Come on," I said, threading my hand through Dawson's elbow on the side opposite from his injury. "How do you feel?"

"It stings like hell. Can't fucking believe I did that."

"What happened?"

"I left a few things under the porch over the summer. Hell if I know why I decided to deal with it tonight."

I was quiet, uncertain of what else to say. I told myself he would be okay. He *had* to be okay. Copperhead bites didn't usually kill unless someone had an unusual reaction to them.

It didn't matter what I told myself. I was scared and worried for Dawson and didn't like seeing him in pain. That worry smashed up against the confusing feelings I'd been carrying inside ever since our last night together.

I practically dragged him down the path to the lodge. Jackson was waiting at the back door, illuminated by the light above it.

As usual, Jackson was all business when it came to anything emergent. As soon as we reached him, he held the door open and gestured us through. I had to force myself to let go of Dawson's arm. His eyes met mine as I stepped back, and for a moment, the distance fell away between us.

Then he was turning away as Jackson pulled him into a small room beside Dani's office.

"Let's take a look. We need to get you to the hospital just to be safe. Wade'll be here any minute, so I'll clean it while we wait," Jackson said.

I wanted to stay so badly, yet there was nothing for me to do. I stood there in the hallway, practically bouncing on my feet with the urge to follow them into the room. I needed to stay sane and not do anything stupid. As I stood there waiting, Wade came in from the front. "Where'd Jackson take Dawson?"

I gestured to the room by Dani's office. Wade stepped in, his voice carrying to me. "I'll drive. You guys ready?"

When they filed out, Dawson's skin pale, I swallowed against the emotion thickening in my throat. "Do you guys need me to do anything?"

When Jackson shook his head, I nodded, not sure what else to say. Watching as they walked out, I told myself I didn't need to get my hopes up again. All over a snakebite. "Can you call, and let me know if he's okay?" I asked Wade as he passed by.

"Of course," came his easy reply.

I waited until the taillights of the emergency vehicle disappeared down the drive before I left. The ache in my heart throbbed with every step on my way back to my cabin.

Chapter Twenty-Three

DAWSON

My wrist and hand throbbed with a dull, beating pain. Beyond being flat pissed off at myself for being so fucking stupid as to reach under my porch in the darkness, the only thing I could think about was Evie.

The moment I'd seen her come running up the path, my emotions slammed into each other, pressing tight together before expanding abruptly. I'd been doing my damnedest and working like a wild man to avoid her.

Seeing her had split all the feelings I'd been trying to hold at bay wide open again. Her concerned gaze, the feel of her hand curled around my elbow, the arch of her brow, the curve of her lips—all the small things that made me miss her so fucking much.

I just got bit by a snake and didn't even care. My head was pounding, and I was exhausted. I had Jackson here being all practical, and Wade driving us to the hospital

"I don't need to go to the hospital, guys. Just give me some ibuprofen, and I'll be fine."

Jackson was in the middle of dabbing antiseptic over the two puncture marks and looked up, arching a brow. "We're going to the hospital. Just to clear you. They'll probably take a look and tell you to monitor it."

I didn't want to go to the hospital. I wanted to go find Evie. I wanted to tell her I was sorry for being a fucking idiot. Everything hit me so abruptly, my emotions were almost pummeling me with clarity.

This snakebite was just a nuisance. Unfortunately for me, I had two friends who gave a shit and weren't going to let me blow it off.

"I'm not gonna die from this fucking bite."

Jackson eyed me. "Just get it checked. You have no idea if you're going to have a reaction." His gaze shifted to Wade, ignoring me. "Van outside?"

Against my preference, I was hustled into the emergency vehicle, not that we needed it. Over the next few hours, I was checked out, the puncture site was disinfected thoroughly, and I was given some prescription-strength ibuprofen to help with the swelling. The whole thing started after ten o'clock at night. I wasn't going to fess up, but I knew what had me so distracted and led me to randomly decide to clean out my summer gear from under the porch in the dark.

I didn't want to think, and the only way to keep from thinking was to keep busy. Flipping through the channels hadn't kept my mind off Evie, so late-night cleaning had seemed just the thing.

Trying to wrestle against my feelings for Evie was practically a full-time job and was wearing me out. Now, I simply wanted to see her. When they finally let me go with orders to monitor the swelling and pain and call if it didn't improve, Wade drove us back to the lodge and walked me to my cabin.

"You need anything else, man?" he asked as I pushed the door open.

"Nope, I'm all set."

When he was quiet for a minute, I sensed he wanted to

say something else, but he apparently thought better of it and nodded. "Call me if you need anything."

"Will do." Watching as he walked into the darkness, I turned and closed the door behind him. I sank my hips onto the end of my bed and glanced at the clock above the door. It was past midnight, and I wanted to go see Evie. Not because I wanted her to take care of me, but because I craved being near her.

It didn't seem too practical, or fair, to go banging on her door now. She'd been coming home from work when she saw me. I didn't even like thinking about the fact that I'd been paying more than usual attention to her schedule. I hated how aware I was of everything about her. I knew I'd hurt her, and I hated that too.

Although I was still leery about the occasional darkness that claimed me—the brutal clarity that struck me tonight was I didn't want to regret my lack of courage about her. If I didn't tell her how I felt, I knew beyond any doubt that letting her go would rank as one of my biggest regrets. I couldn't even fathom feeling anything close to the way I felt about her for anyone else. Maybe I would suck at this, but I had to give it a chance. I wasn't even letting myself screw it up.

I barely slept that night. My wrist hurt like hell, and I tossed and turned with thoughts of Evie spinning on a loop. Ibuprofen took the edge off the pain, but that was about it. Come morning, I inspected the area while I was showering. My hand was swollen on the outer edge of my lower palm and wrist on the back. The bruising was a mottled purple, yellow, and green.

Whether it was rational or not, I decided to try to find Evie this morning. As I stood outside her door, my heart kicked against my ribs hard enough to make me feel a little sick. This was my own doing. I'd never been afraid of a woman before. I didn't suppose it was fear of Evie specifically. It was fear of seeing the pain I had put in her eyes.

After I knocked, I waited just long enough that I thought perhaps I'd missed her. But then, I heard footsteps. My heart started beating so hard I wouldn't have been shocked if I cracked a rib.

The door swung open, and Evie stood there. Her hair was damp and drying around her shoulders. My eyes coasted over her—absorbing the way her brows arched like wings, the curve of her cheek, and the slight tilt to her lips. I wanted to see her lopsided smile so fiercely it was almost a visceral pain.

"Hey, I was hoping to talk to you," I said quickly.

Her mouth opened and closed, and her cheeks flushed before going white again. "Are you okay?" she asked sharply.

"Yeah," I replied, lifting my wrist. "It's sore, but I'm fine. That's not what I wanted to talk about."

"We don't have anything else to talk about, Dawson. I have to go to work." She reached to the side, shrugging into a jacket she pulled off the hook by the door and grabbing her purse.

She dashed past me so quickly, she stumbled slightly. When I caught her arm, she shook me free immediately. "I'm glad you're okay," she said quickly before hurrying away.

I wanted to chase after her so badly, but I had to forcibly order myself not to. I needed to figure out a way to get her to listen, but it wasn't going to work if I was pushy and demanding, especially not when she had somewhere she needed to be. Glancing at my aching wrist, I sighed and turned to walk down to the lodge. I could at least grab some breakfast.

Minutes later, I stepped through the back door into the staff kitchen. Warmth washed over me in contrast to the cool and crisp autumn morning outside. Dani was pulling the coffeepot out with a mug in hand. She glanced over when I came in the door.

"Morning, Dawson," she called.

Evie was nowhere to be found, but then, she was probably already up front in the restaurant.

"Mornin', Dani," I called in return as I strode over to the counter, reaching for a mug on the shelf above the coffeepot. "How's it going?"

"Busy. How's your wrist?" she asked, stepping to my side as I took the coffeepot she handed over and filled the mug.

"Sore, but I'm fine."

Dani narrowed her eyes. "Are you working today?"

Shifting my shoulders to loosen them, I shrugged. "Maybe."

Dani rolled her eyes. "You are such a man."

"Uh, I *am* a man, so that only stands to reason. How late is Evie working today?"

Dani arched a brow before pausing to take a sip of coffee, making me wait for her answer. "She's here for the breakfast and lunch shift. Why is it any business of yours?"

I knew without knowing that Evie must've spoken to Dani about us. Regardless of the details, Dani likely had an opinion of her own. Heading her off, I said, "I fucked up. You're welcome to share your opinion about it." Turning, I leaned my hips against the counter and took a sip of my black coffee, the bitterness suited to my mood.

Dani sighed softly. "You did fuck up. For what it's worth, I told her I thought you really liked her, and that I didn't think it was just about fun for you."

Her words bit sharply. The dull ache along the back of my wrist throbbed deeply. The pain was akin to that in my heart. And it was all my own damn fault.

I gulped my coffee and held Dani's gaze even though I wanted to look away. "She thinks it was just fun?" I asked. Dani's face softened as she nodded slowly. "Fuck," I muttered, just as the door to the restaurant kitchen swung open and Evie hurried through. She'd braided her hair, the braid swinging as she jogged to the storage pantry.

Simply seeing her sent a sharp, burning pain through my heart while I felt cold everywhere else.

"Need some help?" Dani called as she set her mug on the counter behind her and walked briskly to the pantry.

I couldn't hear Evie's reply, just the murmur of her voice. A few seconds later, she was hurrying back out, carrying a large can with Dani right behind her. Evie's eyes locked with mine, and the look there sent chills through me. I saw nothing but hurt mingled with anger in her gaze. She quickly shuttered it and looked away.

I waited a few moments longer after they both disappeared into the front, hoping Dani would return so I could ask her advice, but she didn't. As usual, she was swept into the morning. A glance out the windows told me the parking lot was full, so I knew the restaurant was busy.

Coffee in hand, I decided to search out Jackson. I needed something to distract me from Evie. The fear that I'd lost her for good had my heart aching and a sense of panic churning in my gut.

Chapter Twenty-Four

DAWSON

"Come again?" Jackson asked, looking at me. He held a massive gray rabbit with floppy ears in his arms.

"I need some advice about Evie," I repeated, feeling beyond foolish.

Jackson turned and set the rabbit onto a stainless-steel examination table. Angling back to face me, he rested his hips against it and stroked the rabbit's back. "Well, this is a first," he finally said with a glint of humor in his eyes.

"The first and only," I said flatly.

Given how prone I was to teasing, I didn't think I could be too bitter about him teasing me. At that moment, there were footsteps out in the hallway. A few seconds later, Lucas appeared in the doorway.

"Hey, guys. Checking on the schedule for today. We've got three hikes scheduled, and a bunch of roofing supplies just arrived for those cabins," he explained.

Jackson nodded. "The roofing supplies can wait. I've got appointments in the clinic today." He looked at me. "Think you can handle a hike?"

"Of course."

Lucas looked puzzled. "You okay?"

"I'm fine. Got bit by a copperhead last night."

"Well, damn. Let me see."

I extended my injured hand forward while I sipped my coffee with the other. Lucas eyed it. The bruising wasn't pretty.

"Why are you working today?" he asked when he looked up.

"Because I fucking need something to do."

Lucas, ever unflappable and even-tempered, hitched his brows.

"He's cranky, and now he needs advice," Jackson offered, his tone dry.

I glared at him. "I wasn't looking for group therapy."

Lucas looked back and forth between us, the barest hint of a smile kicking up one corner of his mouth.

"Hey, you offered me unsolicited advice about Shay, and it was on the money. I can return the favor," Jackson cut in.

My chest was tight, but I managed to grin as I glanced at them and shook my head. "Well, I guess you two are better than anyone else. What the fuck do I do?"

"Where do things stand?" Lucas asked, getting directly to the point.

I looked at the rabbit, the one creature in the room I didn't feel would judge me. The rabbit simply stared back, leaning his head into Jackson's knuckles as he scratched behind an ear.

"I don't know. Things got pretty intense. I wasn't sure how to deal with it, so I backed off, and now she won't talk to me. Dani said Evie thought it was all just fun for me."

Jackson's gaze flicked from me to Lucas, and he shook his head slowly. "That's definitely not good. Unless fun *is* all you're after with Evie."

Lucas's gaze was sympathetic. Despite that, he was blunt. "What did you expect her to think? Don't take this the wrong way, but that's the impression you cultivate. If I didn't know you the way I do and from dealing with a few life or death emergencies together, I might think you were a shallow guy. I know there's more to you than that, but it's something you have to deal with."

Rolling my head side to side, I glanced at the rabbit again. The rabbit had nothing to offer. "Fuck," I muttered. Pausing, I drained my coffee. "How do I fix it?"

"You have to tell her how you feel," Jackson said flatly.

"She'll barely talk to me."

Lucas nodded slowly. "You're just gonna have to keep trying if she means that much to you."

"I'd make damn sure you're clear on how important she is to you. I'm not an expert, but it's not a good idea to string someone along unless you're clear about how you feel," Jackson added.

"I love her. I know that much." I leaned against the wall behind me and sighed, bouncing my heel lightly against the baseboard.

"This shit is not easy," Lucas said. "Are you sure you should be working today, anyway?"

Glancing down at my wrist, I looked back up. "It hurts, but the last thing I want to do is be bored today."

Footsteps approached in the hall, and Shay appeared in the doorway. Her blond ponytail swung back and forth as her eyes bounced between us. "Geez, is there a staff meeting I didn't know about?"

Jackson chuckled, his gaze warming as he looked at her. "No. But Dandy's owner will be here to pick him up shortly," he replied, stroking his hand over the rabbit's back.

"Dandy?" Lucas queried.

Shay smiled. "The rabbit's name is Dandy."

"Ah," Lucas said slowly. "Is Valentina busy?"

Shay's wide smile was nearly gleeful. "She just finished up a teleconference with one of our suppliers about some accounting discrepancies. You can find her in her office."

Lucas grinned. "Well, I'd best be going." Glancing at

Jackson, he said, "I'll take the shorter hike and then rendezvous with you this afternoon to deal with the roofing supplies. Sound like a plan?"

At Jackson's nod, he left, his footsteps moving swiftly down the hall. A voice called Shay's name, and she spun away, leaving me behind with Jackson and Dandy.

Knotted up inside, I wanted to ask Jackson if this awful feeling would go away, yet I didn't have it in me. I sensed I already knew the answer. Unless I could sort this out with Evie, I had a feeling the weight I felt would only grow heavier.

Chapter Twenty-Five

EVIE

I tipped back my strawberry margarita, taking a long swallow. "All right, boys. Let's do this," I said as I set the drink down on the narrow counter running along the wall beside the pool table.

Reaching for the pool stick, I stepped toward the table, glancing around at the balls strewn across the green felt surface.

"You think you can beat that sweet shot?" Wade asked.

"Maybe," I countered.

Adjusting the stick in my hands, I leaned over and drew back slightly, the cool wood sliding through my palm as I tapped the cue ball. It rolled into another ball, setting into motion my perfectly placed cascade, which ended with a ball slipping neatly into the corner pocket.

Wade whistled under his breath. "Damn. That was good."

I straightened and smiled. "It was, wasn't it?"

As I turned to reach for my margarita, my eyes landed on Dawson as he walked across the bar. My smile faded inside, but I kept it plastered on my face. There was no way in hell I was going to let anyone see just how much it hurt for me to see him. Taking a gulp of my margarita, I couldn't help but notice the female eyes following Dawson through the bar. I had no doubt some of the women looking at him had enjoyed his talents in the bedroom.

I wasn't bitter. Not at all. I didn't miss his kisses, the feel of his body warm against me, or that look in his silver-gray eyes. The look that made me feel as if I was the only woman in the world to him.

I drained my margarita and glanced back at Wade who'd just made another sweet shot. "I need another drink. Whoever wants to take my shot can have it."

I didn't wait to see what happened, setting my pool stick in the rack and striding to the bar, the heels of my cowboy boots striking loudly on the wide plank flooring underneath.

Leaning against the bar, I lifted my hand to catch the bartender's attention. Delilah glanced my way as she filled a pint glass with beer. I held up my now empty margarita glass, and she nodded in acknowledgment. After she finished pulling a few drafts for some of the guys on the far side of the bar, she came over to me.

"Another strawberry margarita?"

"Yes, please."

"Coming right up."

She turned away, responding to a request from yet another man who approached the bar. I felt Dawson's presence before I saw him. I took a breath, ordering my pulse not to go crazy, but that was a complete waste of effort. I couldn't be near Dawson, or even think about being near him, without my body going haywire.

"I was hoping to talk to you," he said as he stopped beside me. The gruff sound of his voice sent a frisson of electricity chasing down my spine. Part of me was near frantic *not* to look at him while another part craved the sight of him.

Everything hurt. My heart, my confidence. It was like a

physical ache. To make matters worse, I'd hardly slept last night. Another sleepless night on the heels of far too many just like it. Sleep was a cruel tease for me lately. I couldn't help but worry about him. I'd had to tell myself a few too many times to stop. Restless, I'd climbed out of bed in the middle of the night to look up copperhead bites online.

According to the internet, unless someone was very young or old, they were unlikely to even need medical treatment beyond monitoring—unless they were highly allergic and had an unusual reaction.

As hale and hearty as Dawson was, I knew that was extremely unlikely, but it didn't matter. Not deep in the night when my mind lingered on every worst-case scenario possible. The loneliness of nighttime worrying was intense. It felt as if I were truly all alone with nothing to keep my thoughts on a sane track. Worries spun in endless circles.

That explained my irritation when Dawson showed up on my porch the next morning. He wanted to talk after blowing me off for weeks.

With this mash-up of thoughts tumbling through my mind, I stared at him. His dark blond hair was mussed as if he'd run a hand through it a few too many times. Weariness was evident in the lines of tension on his face.

My eyes flicked to his wrist, and I saw the swelling had gone down substantially from last night, but the whole area was discolored in a mottled yellow, green, and purple. My gaze swung up, absorbing the strong lines of his features—that square jaw with a shadow of stubble, and his sensual lips so often tipped into a teasing half-grin. Tonight, there wasn't even a hint of humor visible in his expression.

"How are you?" I asked.

"I've been better. If you're asking about this ..." He paused, lifting his wrist and twisting it side to side. "It's sore, but that's it."

Relief washed through me as I nodded. "I'm glad you're

okay," I managed. My heart gave an almost painful thump. I wanted to cry.

"I was hoping we could talk," he repeated, his voice low.

Just then, Delilah arrived with my drink. "Here you go. Put it on your tab?"

Distracted, I looked her way and nodded, then grabbed my drink and took a gulp. Our next interruption came in the form of Sheila Wilkins. She was beautiful with straight dark hair, delicate features, and legs that went on forever.

"Hey, Dawson," Sheila said, her voice coquettish. She paused beside him, brushing her hair off her shoulder.

I'd gone to high school with Sheila. She'd been the head cheerleader, beautiful, socially deft, and a bit of a bully when she felt like it. She hid it well, but every now and then, her social guard fell. I'd been one of her targets for a brief period. We'd been stuck together in biology class with assigned seating. Unlike other classes, we shared tables with each other in biology. As a result, I hadn't been able to avoid her.

Unfortunately for me, Sheila was not a great student. When she got caught cheating on a test, and I refused to cover for her, she started mocking me in the locker room. Ninth grade was when my late bloomer stage was at its worst, and only months after Krista had died.

Sheila didn't even bother to look at me just now. If I could've picked a worse time and a worse woman to flirt with Dawson in my presence, I would've been hard pressed to find one.

Of course, he knew none of this history because he hadn't gone to high school with us. I would've been willing to bet a million dollars that Dawson had spent more than one night in her bed. Dawson glanced her way, offering nothing more than a tight smile. "Hey, Sheila."

"Long time, no see," she said, stepping closer and sliding her hand through his elbow where he had his thumb hooked over the edge of his pocket.

"If you don't mind, I'm busy right now," he said, his tone flat and polite.

I purposely looked away because I didn't want to deal with the look I knew I would see in Sheila's eyes. I knew I wasn't the girl I had once been. In fact, I enjoyed flirting, and I didn't even think I was an ugly duckling anymore.

Yet somehow Sheila lit up every single one of my insecurity buttons. I felt like one of those old giant handheld phone receivers was pinned to my chest, and Sheila had her middle finger on a button smack in the center.

Abruptly, I decided I didn't want to watch the rest of this interaction. Another thing I understood quite well about Sheila was her tendency to be bitchy and competitive. I had no interest in being on the receiving end of whatever bullshit she might pull if she thought something was going on between Dawson and me.

"I have to go," I said, turning and walking away as quickly as I could, threading through the tables to the pool table in the corner.

I heard Dawson say my name from behind me, but I ignored it. I needed the safety blanket of an audience to protect me from him trying to pursue a conversation with me right now. Unfortunately for me, he came right over to the pool table after whatever the hell he said to Sheila to shake free from her.

There were enough mutual friends there that I could keep ignoring him, and I did. On my fourth margarita, I missed a shot and lost my balance when I straightened.

"Think you may need to call it a night," Grace said.

"Why?" I countered.

Grace wasn't my best friend for nothing. "You've had too much to drink."

I stumbled a little as I tried to step away from the table.

"You're a little too tipsy now," she added, her arm sliding around my shoulders as she deftly removed the pool stick from my hands and handed it to someone.

"I can take her home."

At the sound of Dawson's voice, I spun to face him, losing my balance and bumping against the wall and back into Grace. Grace lived up to her name and graciously steadied me on my feet.

"I don't want a fucking ride from you," I retorted, my words coming out slurred as I wagged my finger at him.

Suddenly, the numbing effects of the alcohol fled, and I almost started to cry. Dawson looked pained, his eyes sweeping over me and convincing me in my drunken state that he might actually care.

"Evie, for God's sake, you can't drive," Dawson replied, his tone so reasonable my emotions swung from pain to anger in a flash.

"Fuck you," I said, not caring that we had quite the audience, which included most of our friends as well as everyone nearby in the bar.

"Evie, I just offered to give you a ride. It's not a big deal."

Dawson started to move away, but I reached out, grabbing for his hand. When I heard his breath through his teeth, I realized I had snatched at his injured hand. "Oh God, I'm sorry."

Dropping his hand quickly, I stumbled again. Thrown off balance, this time I fell into him. His arms curled around me. "Hey, it's okay," he said softly.

Close to him, I suddenly didn't want to move. Instead, I let my head fall against his chest. "I'm so stupid," I muttered. "Why'd you have to go and trick me?"

His hand slid down my back in a soothing pass. "I think we should save this conversation for later," he murmured, bending low so his mouth was close to my ear.

I nudged my shoulder into his chest. "You're the one who wanted to talk. So let's talk."

"Now's not the best time. We've got an audience. Let me take you home."

Between the alcohol and the mess of my feelings, just a commotion inside, I couldn't be reasonable. Not at all.

"No," I said mulishly. "You've been ignoring me."

I finally looked up at him, and my heart felt split wide open. I thought maybe I'd stitched it together somehow by sheer force of will. But no.

The moment I looked in his eyes, I remembered the look in them when he was buried deep inside me and what it felt like to believe—no matter how foolish—that what we had was something more than just sex.

"Evie," Dawson began, his voice tight.

Grace cut in. "Evie, honey, I don't think you really want to do this here."

I swung my eyes to her and shook my head wildly. "I'm not leaving. He wanted to talk, so we're gonna talk."

Then I heard Sheila's voice. "So the rumors are true?" She stopped beside us, looking from me to Dawson. "You're in over your head, girl. Dawson is way out of your league."

"Sheila." Dawson's voice held a sharp edge.

She ignored him. Her eyes flicked back and forth between us again. "Her? You can't even tell me you think she's cute. She's—"

I burst out laughing, cutting off whatever she meant to say.

"You fucking bitch! That's rich. All you can do is sleep around. You've been doing it for so fucking long all the guys know that's all you're good for," Grace said, leaning forward and pressing her finger on Sheila's chest. It was glorious. Stepping back, she let her gaze travel up and down Sheila. "Back the fuck off."

I wasn't sure what Sheila expected, but I was pretty sure it wasn't this. She looked around, likely hoping for someone to come to her defense, but no one did.

Her complexion was mottled pink and white when she looked back at Dawson and me. "Whatever."

Dawson held her gaze. “Sheila, don’t you ever talk about Evie like that again and leave me the hell alone.”

Throughout this interaction, Dawson held me in the shelter of his arms. Somewhere along the way, I had curled my fingers around the hem of this T-shirt and slipped my other arm around his waist. He was warm and strong, and I didn’t want to go anywhere.

Sheila didn’t reply and spun away, her footsteps loud as she strode across the bar.

“Good riddance,” Dani said.

I’d lost track of who all was here. I peered out from Dawson’s arms to see Wade with his eyes tracking Sheila’s progress out of the bar. Jackson was leaning against the end of the pool table with an arm around Shay’s shoulders. Dani had her hands on her hips, her eyes pinned to Sheila as if making sure she actually left.

Grace was still beside me. Her eyes caught mine. “I’m sorry, it had to be said. She was a fucking bitch to you in high school, and she’s been a bitch to plenty others since then. There’s a reason she has no female friends.”

My vision blurred as the tears pressing hot in my eyes finally welled up, and a rough sob came out. Dawson rubbed my back in soothing circles. “Hey, hey, it’s okay.”

Looking up, I saw him glance at Grace as if uncertain what to do. Grace shrugged. “There’s some history there, but I don’t think that’s why she’s crying.”

She stepped closer to us. “I can give you a ride home. Just tell me what you need.” Dawson started to speak, and Grace’s eyes flicked to him. “This needs to be her call tonight,” she said carefully.

“Dawson can take me home,” I finally said between sniffles. I uncurled my hand from his shirt to swipe at the tears rolling down my cheeks.

I wasn’t ready to talk, but no matter what came of it, I needed to be close to Dawson right now.

Chapter Twenty-Six

DAWSON

Evie was drunk. Messy drunk. After the scene in Lost Deer Bar, I managed to get her outside with just about all our friends following. I didn't mind their presence so much, but I focused on getting her home. I'd relinquished any hope we were going to talk tonight because she was definitely too drunk.

Trying to get her in my truck would've been difficult if it weren't for her being so lightweight. After I opened the door, she tried twice to climb in, her foot slipping each time. She elbowed me away the third time, and I caught her the next time. Lifting her, I said, "Let's just get you home. This is the quickest way."

I eased her in, leaning around her and ignoring her sweet, musky scent as I buckled her seat belt. When I met her gaze, her blue eyes were hazy. Her lips curled into one of her endearing, lopsided smiles.

I couldn't resist. Leaning forward, I brushed my lips over hers. I wanted our kiss to be so much more than that, but it wasn't the time. When I drew back, she sighed. "I missed you." A tear rolled down her cheek.

Oh God. I didn't really know how to do tears. I cupped her cheek, catching her tear with my thumb. "It's going to be okay," I said, feeling helpless and hating it.

Evie shook her head as more tears rolled down her cheeks. She sniffled loudly as I stood there, internally fumbling with how the hell to respond to this. Tears all on their own were enough of a challenge, but throw in Evie being drunk and me only recently and quite painfully coming to terms with being in love with her, and I had *no* idea what to do.

Quite obviously, we needed to talk. Hell, I was the one who wanted to talk tonight. But not like this, not when she was drunk enough she might not remember a thing I said.

"Easy for you to say it's going to be okay," she said, her words soft and frayed.

Although it was dark, the lights in the parking lot were bright. I didn't think the illumination was meant to break my heart just a little more at seeing the pain held in Evie's eyes.

"I'm sorry. I know I screwed up. You're right, it's easy for me to say. I'm just trying to convince myself."

"Convince yourself of what?"

"That maybe you're in love with me too."

Evie's eyes widened. She hiccupped and sniffled, smearing her palm across her damp cheeks. "What?"

"Seeing as I'm in love with you, it'll be okay if maybe you returned the feeling."

She stared at me, her mouth falling open with another hiccup and a loud sniffle. She tried to punch me in the shoulder. It was painless, and she barely made contact, but I didn't miss the anger flashing in her eyes.

"Why'd you blow me off?" she demanded.

I didn't have a good answer, but I had the answer. If necessary, we would just replay this conversation when she was sober.

"Like I told you, shit with my dad messed with my head.

I never thought I'd get serious with anyone. When I went home to see my mom, she said sometimes I remind her of my dad because I get depressed." Pausing, I took a breath, trying to marshal my nerves to get through the rest of this. These were all things I had known so well, yet I never spoke out loud about them.

Evie went still. She wasn't quiet, not with the sniffles and the occasional hiccup, but I forged ahead. "So I just thought it was better if I kept my distance before I screwed things up, or before you saw that side of me."

I felt raw and exposed in a way I had never let myself be vulnerable before. Between sniffles, she reached out and grabbed my hand, almost missing. I caught her hand in mine. Tears rolled down her cheeks as she spoke. "That's crazy. I would never care about that. We all go through shit, Dawson."

Although her speech was a little slurred, her words were so earnest that my throat tightened as emotion barreled into me. Swallowing through it, I nodded. "I know. I didn't say it was rational. Then I got bit by that snake, and it made me think."

Abruptly, she gasped, glancing down at our hands. "It's okay. That's the good one," I offered with a chuckle.

A car door slammed nearby, reminding me we were in the middle of a busy parking lot. The door to the bar opened with voices carrying out.

"Let's get you home, okay?"

Evie's eyes were glistening with tears as she searched my face. After a moment, she nodded. She had yet to release my hand, and I glanced down at it. "Going to need this," I said, giving her hand a gentle squeeze.

She hiccupped and uncurled her fingers from mine. Stepping back, I closed the door and rounded the front of the truck to climb into the driver's seat. I drove us back to the lodge, my headlights illuminating the frost, a layer of glitter across the landscape hinting at the winter to come.

We didn't talk further on the drive home. I felt almost lightheaded, a rush of emotion coming in the aftermath at the reality of voicing my feelings out loud. As if that made them more real, almost like casting a spell. I couldn't take it back now. I didn't mind that Evie hadn't repeated the same. Although I wondered if she did love me.

When I parked and glanced over, I found her sound asleep, so I carried her inside. As I lifted her into my arms, she stayed asleep, letting out a hiccup followed by a soft sigh when she tucked her head into my shoulder. I carried her through the trees to my cabin.

Chapter Twenty-Seven

DAWSON

It took a bit of wrangling, but I got Evie down to her underwear and dragged one of my T-shirts over her head. I didn't think she would want to wake up in her jeans and cowboy boots. As she'd been doing since the day I first clapped eyes on her, she tested my will.

She had on this ridiculous excuse for a bra—sheer cream silk and lace with her nipples peeking at me and panties to match. Ruthlessly, I yanked my T-shirt over her head. She sighed in response. After I tucked her under the covers, I took a quick shower, cold enough to take the edge off my inconvenient arousal.

For the first time in weeks, I got to fall asleep with Evie warm and soft beside me. I would take it. Every fucking night if I could have it.

Dawn crept into the room by degrees, a silvery light coming through the window because I'd forgotten to close the shades last night. I woke up with my palm cupping Evie's sweet bottom and her breasts pressed against my side. My pulse kicked up the moment my consciousness flickered to life. Opening my eyes, I turned my head, taking in the sweet sight of her.

Dark lashes brushed against her cheeks. Her breath came in steady, even gusts. Lifting a hand, I brushed her hair away from her face, savoring the way it slid soft and silky through my fingers. I could watch her sleep all day. Her face, usually mobile and slightly tense, relaxed in sleep. I let my thumb trace down the slope of her cheek to her crooked mouth.

God, I wanted to kiss her so fiercely, I felt as if I were holding back a fire with my bare hands.

Evie's eyes opened. She was utterly still as she looked at me. "Oh." Her voice had a rasp to it like it did whenever she woke up.

For a moment, I simply basked in the knowledge of being with her. I felt like a cat luxuriating in the sun. In this case, Evie was the sun and just for me.

"Good morning."

She swallowed, smiling sleepily before announcing, "I have to pee."

The last thing I wanted to do was let her climb out of this bed and remove her delectable curves from my immediate reach. But I was a practical man, if nothing else.

"In that case, you should probably pee."

A tinge of pink washed over her cheeks, and she shifted against me as she rolled out from under the covers.

On second thought, the sight of Evie walking into the bathroom where I had a nice view of her sweet bottom wasn't such a bad plan after all. The door closed behind her, and within a moment or two, I heard the toilet flush followed by the faucet running. Much to my satisfaction, she returned and crawled back under the covers with me.

"It really is fall. It's chilly," she said.

I could feel the pebbled peaks of her nipples against my side when she burrowed into me. "Fall is definitely here," I murmured in reply, pulling her tight against me.

I wanted to get busy. Right now. But I also knew she might not remember a single thing from our conversation in the truck last night. I shifted on the pillow slightly, adjusting an elbow behind my head and noticing my other wrist was only mildly sore. "So tell me, do you remember anything from last night?"

She rolled slightly to the side, angling to look at my face. I was instantly disappointed because she wasn't mashed against me anymore. The lines of her face tightened a bit. "I remember I was mad at you and kind of made a scene at the bar. I remember crying in your truck, and I think ..." She paused, uncertainty flickering in her eyes.

"I told you I love you. In case you forgot that part," I offered, my voice coming out gruff.

Her cheeks had more than a tinge of pink now. She stared at me, her eyes blinking wide. "You told me you love me? Last night?"

I bit my lip to keep from laughing. She looked so adorable. I also knew the urge to laugh was a familiar defense. I wanted to tease because I was terrified of this moment.

A tear spilled out and slipped down her cheek. "Hey, hey, I didn't mean to make you cry," I said, tightening my arm around her.

She shook her head. "No, no. I'm not sad. That's a happy tear."

My befuddlement must've been apparent because she smiled slowly. "You don't cry when you're really happy?"

I shook my head. "Can't say that's ever happened."

She buried her face against my chest, her shoulders shaking with a few giggles. When she lifted her head, her eyes were still wet with tears, but I got one of her lopsided smiles. My heart drummed wildly in my chest.

"I can't believe I don't remember the first time you told me. You kind of broke my heart," she said, her gaze sobering.

"I didn't mean to hurt you," I replied, wishing there was a way to show just how deeply I meant that.

She moved closer, her fingers tracing a circle on my chest. "I know. Well, I didn't really know." When she shifted again, her knee brushed against my quite obvious arousal. When her eyes met mine, they darkened. "I think we should talk later."

"Ignore it. I'd rather talk first and clear the air," I said, trying to sound firm.

"I'd rather have make-up sex," she said with a sly grin as she planted her lips on mine.

I needed no further convincing. With her warm, plush lips teasing me and her sassy tongue flicking inside to tangle with mine, I forgot what I thought we needed to talk about.

She shimmied over me, straddling my lap and letting out a soft hum. I fucking loved the sounds she made.

With Evie, I was learning it was the little things that told the story of just what love was. I couldn't remember the sounds any other woman made. I'd had my share of fun and had nothing to complain about. But with Evie, every single detail was seared into my memory on a visceral level—the little sounds she made, the way she bit her lip when she was cresting the wave of a climax, the way one of her eyes was a little wider than the other, the crook in her nose, and her lopsided smile.

Evie was it. *All* of her was *everything* for me.

I knew no matter what, if I could have her, no one else could ever claim my heart as thoroughly as she had. I shifted up on the pillows, curling my hands around her hips and holding her still. I was about to go off at any second.

We weren't even naked yet. She still had on those ridiculous panties, so tempting I didn't want to ruin them but knew I would. I was sure that cream silk and lace had been made to drive me personally insane. Sweet heaven. Taking a breath, I gripped her hips when she rocked over the ridge of my cock.

"Fuck, Evie. Hold still," I bit out.

She surprised me by obeying instantly. As I looked into her eyes, my heart set to drumming again. My pulse went off the charts in response to Evie's mere existence—an elemental desire. There was that, and then what happened to my heart when I actually let myself believe she might feel the same way I did.

Her eyes were wide and dark, a hint of that playfulness that was so her contained within.

"I love you," I murmured.

For some reason, I needed to say it just now to make sure she knew how true it was. If my heart was a compass, Evie was my true north, south, east, and west. All directions pointed to her. It didn't matter where I went, she was the homing device for my heart.

The uncertainty I'd seen in her eyes last night in the bar when Sheila threw her barbs flickered again.

"Don't," I said flatly.

"Don't what?"

Her voice had a sleepy husk to it. I wanted to hug her, and fuck her, and sleep with her, and never forget the ray of sunshine she cast into my life.

"That look." I could feel the sweet heat of her pussy through the thin layers of silk and cotton between us. "The same one you got last night. I don't know what it is, but I don't like when I see it."

Her lashes swept against her cheeks when her gaze dropped. Her breasts pushed against my chest as she took a deep breath. When her eyes met mine again, there was a tinge of sadness contained there.

"I'm just not really the kind of girl it seems like you would fall in love with."

"Seeing as I've only been in love once, and it's with you, I beg to differ."

Evie rolled her eyes. "Until I got to know you better, I just thought you were a player. You were never a jerk. I liked to joke around with you, but you didn't know me. Not really. Remember how I told you my twin sister died?"

My heart physically ached at the depth of pain that dashed through her eyes because I couldn't even imagine that kind of loss. I knew how I felt about my brother, so I could only guess her connection to her twin sister was all that much more powerful.

At my nod, she continued, "Well, that happened the summer before I started high school. I wasn't really doing well at all then. High school was hard enough on its own, but I missed Krista, and Sheila was a bitch. She teased me and bullied me for a year before she moved on the next year. I guess her one saving grace was she didn't stick with any one target for too long."

I suddenly wanted to kick Sheila's ass. I'd never laid a hand on a woman—or man, for that matter—in my life, but to think someone would go after Evie like that hit me hard.

I didn't know what Evie saw in my eyes, but she cocked her head to the side, shaking it with a rueful smile. "It was years ago. I'm older and wiser, and mostly over that shitty period of my life. If I hadn't been drunk last night, Sheila couldn't have gotten to me. I'm kind of embarrassed she did. Anyway, my point is, I picture you as one of the popular guys in high school, the kind of guy who would have never looked twice at me."

Biting her lip, she shrugged, her eyes bouncing away from me. Releasing one of her hips, I lifted my hand to cup her chin. Her eyes swung back, holding mine.

"I can see why you might think that. Because of the way my life was growing up, being the class clown was my escape. Don't go thinking I wouldn't have noticed you. I didn't notice much of anyone. My dad was off his rocker on whatever the drug of the week was, and I was dodging his fists. Maybe what you saw the past few years could've given you the impression that I was somebody I wasn't. I won't pretend I was a saint, but I just tried to stay on the surface of everything. The first day I met you, I think I knew you were special, so I teased the hell out of you."

"Is that why I was usually the butt of your worst practical jokes?" she parried, her lips curling in a slow smile.

I shrugged. "I won't pretend I was mature about it. I just wasn't ready for you yet."

She lifted a hand, smoothing her thumb lightly across my brows. The look in her eyes and her sweet smile spun like silk around my heart, lassoing me and holding me tighter and tighter to her.

"I wasn't ready either," she said, her voice catching. She took a shuddery breath. "I love you, you know?"

I'd been prepared to wait, for however long I had to, but I wouldn't lie, my heart nearly cracked a rib at her words. Swallowing through the emotion knotting in my throat, I shook my head. "Can't say that I did. I thought maybe I'd completely screwed up."

"You'll have to try a lot harder to screw up." She tipped her head forward and pressed her lips to mine.

We held still for a few beats, our breaths mingling as she drew back no more than a whisper away. When she rocked her hips slightly, that was it. I fit my mouth over hers and poured weeks of longing into our kiss.

The feel of her silky skin against mine and her soft curves pressing into me lashed at me. I murmured, "I need you."

"I'm yours."

I kept thinking I needed to slow down and savor this, but I couldn't. The fire burned too hot and too bright. I was lost, tossed asunder in this storm of emotion, desire, and fierce need.

Somehow, I got her panties off and threw the T-shirt she'd been wearing to the floor while she dragged my briefs down my legs. Then she was rising up and sinking down over me, sheathing me in her silken core.

The sun still wasn't up when it was over, but I'd lost all

sense of time. We lay there on the bed, our breath coming in heaves, and her pussy clenching around me. We eventually untangled ourselves, and I tugged the covers over us.

When a ray of sun angled across the bed, Evie trailed her fingertips in a lazy path across my chest.

Chapter Twenty-Eight

EVIE

Weeks passed, and I was in a haze of bliss. I still couldn't quite believe Dawson loved me. Late one afternoon, I draped a cape over Valentina's shoulders in the back of the staff kitchen. Valentina had begged me to cut her red curls. Her hair was so glorious it was almost not fair. I reluctantly agreed on the condition that I took no more than an inch.

Valentina sat in the back of the staff kitchen, her feet tucked over the rungs of a stool as I eyed the wild tumble of curls. "Only an inch," she said firmly.

"Yes, ma'am. Shall I gather the clippings and put them in a locket for Lucas?" I teased.

Valentina blushed, and her cheeks went pink as she rolled her eyes. "That's ridiculous."

"Somehow, I doubt Lucas would think so." That earned me another eye roll. "How are things with you two, anyway?"

Valentina pursed her lips as she considered my question. "Good. I think."

"Are you still having hot as hell sex?"

She giggled and nodded when I caught her eyes as I

leaned around her shoulder. I decided I could use her advice. "So tell me, do you think I'm being crazy about Dawson?"

She shook her head firmly, her curls swinging as I lifted a comb off the counter beside us. "How come?" I asked as I carefully began to comb through her curly hair.

"Because of the way he looks at you."

Valentina's words held such confidence. Just as I was about to reply, the door to the hallway opened, and Lucas stepped through.

He looked toward us. I knew what Valentina meant about the way a man looked at someone. The way Lucas looked at her was enough to make me feel as if I'd interrupted a hot and heavy moment.

Lucas had always been the tall, dark, and inscrutable type. At least, in my estimation. But when he looked at Valentina, his eyes cleared as if the sun had just broken through the clouds after days of rain. Oh, and he looked like he wanted to eat her up.

He leaned his shoulder against the wall by the door. "You're getting your hair cut?"

I stepped away, pausing to sip my cup of coffee. Valentina nodded. "Just a trim."

I caught Lucas's gaze and winked. "I promise I won't cut more than an inch."

He chuckled. "Well, thank God for small favors. I was trying to be a good sport, but I love those curls."

Lucas was not a man to say much, so I almost melted on the spot at how sweet his words were. Not for me, but for my friend. I looked at Valentina. "You're stuck with those curls forever."

She smiled, her cheeks blooming pink as Lucas pushed away from the wall and crossed to her quickly, closing the distance between them in a few strides. Leaning down, he cupped her cheek and pressed a quick kiss to her lips. He stepped back swiftly, almost as if the distance was necessary to maintain his control. Considering how totally hot Valentina was, I surmised it was entirely necessary.

"I have a hike this afternoon. Are you coming over tonight?" he asked, the hopefulness in his voice making my heart squeeze for them.

Valentina nodded. "If you want."

Lucas arched a brow. "Of course, I want," he teased.

Valentina and Lucas had only recently got together. They were trying to take things slow for the sake of his daughter. After Rylie's mother died, most of Lucas's life revolved around her. While I commended them for their restraint, it was obvious they were deeply in love.

After Lucas left, I drained my coffee and returned to Valentina's curls. The rich dark shade of red was so gorgeous it was hard to believe it was natural. "You two are so romantic it hurts to watch," I commented as I began combing through her hair.

Valentina shrugged lightly. "Really?"

"Oh my God," I replied, fanning my face and sighing. "Sweet Jesus. One of these days, Lucas is going to set a building on fire with the way he looks at you. It's so hot and sweet."

Valentina took that comment and spun it right back to our conversation before Lucas interrupted us. "That's what I mean about Dawson."

"What? He does *not* look at me that way."

When I glanced around her shoulder as I stepped to her side to begin trimming, her grin was knowing. "Oh yes, he does. He always has. Or at least as long as I've been here. Here's the thing. He covers it up because he's such a tease, but before you two got together, there was his regular teasing, and then what he does with you. You've always been in your own special category for him."

"Oh," I replied as I snipped at the ends of her curls, turning the idea over in my mind.

Though it was hard to believe Valentina when I wasn't

swimming in the currents of self-doubt, if I let myself consider the look in his eyes when we were alone together, I knew how it felt. His gaze washed away the world around us. Everything else fell away in the space we held together.

Dani sent me to Asheville with Dawson, ostensibly to pick up supplies. We were, in fact, picking up supplies for the restaurant and lumber for the cabins Jackson and most of the guys were building before the snow flew. Although we had good reason to go, I sensed she was doing her best to throw us together. Not that she needed to try very hard.

We were spending every night together as it was, but I still had those lingering worries about the weeks when he shut me out and the reasons behind it.

We were driving one of the lodge trucks today, a giant truck with a bench seat. Dawson tugged me to his side as soon as we started driving. With his warm, strong palm curled over my thigh, I was finding it hard to focus.

"You know, you don't have to have your hands on me all the time," I muttered, restlessly shifting my legs. When I glanced up and his silver gaze caught mine, the now familiar desire flickering there, I felt a tug in my belly and squeezed my thighs together.

"Are you complaining?" he countered.

"Not exactly. It's just sometimes I need to focus."

His low chuckle warmed my heart. After we got the lumber, he suggested we grab lunch at Candy's Diner. Seeing as I was starving, and I knew the food was guaranteed to be good, I was happy to go along.

Once we were seated, Dawson glanced over at me. "So what are you getting?"

"What do you recommend?"

"I'm going for her massive everything breakfast. I'm fucking starving."

"What's in the everything breakfast?"

"Bacon, eggs, hash browns, and a side of biscuits and gravy."

"That's what I'm getting."

When a smile slowly stretched across his face, emotion rocked me out of nowhere. There was something so mundane about stopping to get breakfast together. It felt real and true and simple and everything. Just breakfast.

After we ate, Dawson went to the restroom before we left. Candy stopped by our table, holding up a pot of coffee in question. "Oh no, I've had enough for today. Thank you," I said.

She looked at me for a long moment after she lowered the coffeepot. "I hope you know how much you mean to him."

I nodded, my pulse fluttering wildly. "I think I do."

At that moment, he returned to the table, and I took my chance to take a bathroom break. After we left with hugs from Candy and were back in the truck, Dawson glanced over, his gaze suddenly serious.

"She told me to stop being an idiot," he said.

"How are you being an idiot?"

"I explained why I kind of flipped out and kept you at a distance. I was afraid of how much you meant and whether I could be the kind of man you deserve." He idly traced his finger over the curve of the steering wheel.

His lashes brushed against his cheeks when he closed his eyes, and my heart squeezed. The man I had come to know was so much more than what he showed on the surface. He felt things deeply, and because of what he'd gone through, he held everything close inside.

"Dawson, I can't say I understand exactly what you've experienced because we all go through things differently. But I know what it's like to feel the dark side. It's different, I think, than what you've experienced, but after my sister died ..." I paused, needing to take a breath because the pain hit me sharply just then. I'd learned the knife of grief dulled over time, but it was always there. And every so often, it twisted.

He opened his eyes, his gaze clear. I didn't have to explain further. "I know. We've got this, right?"

My heart opened wide. It felt as if the sun was pouring in so brightly I almost couldn't bear the warmth of its blaze. "We do," I said, reaching over to catch his hand.

He squeezed tightly and then unfurled my hand, dropping a kiss in the center of my palm. "If there's one thing I figured out, it's that everything is better with you."

We made out in the truck, right there in the parking lot. We might've pushed the limits a bit too far because a horn nearby had us breaking apart, gasping for air.

EPILOGUE

Evie

A year or so later

I leaned back, the rock surface cool through my jacket. Dawson's warmth emanated from beside me, and I rolled my head sideways to look at him in the moonlight. Because nature had graced him, perhaps too much, in the good looks department, I sighed.

With the moon gilding his hair, I admired the clean lines of his profile, his straight nose, and his chiseled, square jaw. His sensual lips were nature giving a swirl on the mastery of his face.

"You're ridiculous, you know?"

He glanced sideways. In the pearly light, I caught his silver-gray gaze. "How am I ridiculous?" he countered, the teasing tone in his voice making my belly ripple.

A full year had passed, and I still felt as if Dawson had some sort of secret code into every part of my body. With nothing more than a smile, the sound of his voice, or God forbid, his touch, he could send an electric sizzle down my spine and heat spinning through my veins.

I rolled onto my side, adjusting my elbow on the jacket he'd laid on the rock for me. "You're too good looking. God, I hope you lose your hair or something. If not, I'll spend my entire life feeling inadequate."

His grin stretched wider. "Cut that shit out. You're fucking gorgeous."

The thing was, when Dawson said it, I believed it. It wasn't about whether I was objectively, but more the way I felt when held in his ebullient gaze.

"And you're a flatterer and a tease," I countered.

He rolled to his side, mirroring my position so we faced each other in the darkness. This was our last night here at Stolen Hearts Lodge, and we decided to visit the rock where everything had started. I'd come to accept that we'd likely have found our way to each other no matter what, yet the night we ran into each other here had certainly set the universe turning.

"Maybe," he said, lifting a hand and tucking a lock of hair behind my ear. A little shiver chased down my side at the brush of his fingers along the sensitive skin there. "But you're the only one I flatter and tease anymore."

My heart squeezed, and I shifted a little closer, tucking my knees against his. "Mostly. Except for the animals, the guys, and well, everyone."

His low laugh vibrated through me. "Okay, let me clarify. You're the only one I want."

Dawson had turned out to be the best kind of boyfriend. He was ridiculously attentive, and when we were in public, I was half-embarrassed most of the time. Smiling, I dusted a kiss on his cheek and pulled back. "So, you ready?" I asked.

"For what?"

"Moving into our house. It's kind of a big step."

He lifted his shoulder in a small shrug. "Not with you. Everything is easy with you. I have a question."

He said that last bit almost offhandedly, dropping it in so casually, it snagged my attention, and it suddenly felt momentous. I couldn't say why, but I was always fumbling with this echoing feeling that I might lose him somehow. It wasn't because of anything he'd ever done or because of anything horrible some other man had done.

No, rather, I think it was because of the echo of my twin sister's death. Dawson was the only other person I'd been this close to. My connection with him was a different kind of connection—for obvious reasons—yet it contained an intimacy I had never experienced before. My belly tightened in a nervous, spinning anticipation.

As he looked at me, the anxiety started to calm. After we stumbled through the beginning of our relationship, Dawson had become the most stable, centering force in my life. My parents loved me, as did my brother, but I'd been the one in my family who struggled the most in the aftermath of Krista's death. No one quite knew how to help me, so I'd often feel alone, swimming in a grief that almost drowned me at times.

Dawson rarely spoke of it, but he was so one-hundred-percent rock solid *there*. For me.

He shifted, sliding his hand into his pocket and pulling out what looked like a ball of tissue. Upon closer inspection in the darkness, I saw that it was a silk handkerchief.

"Marry me, Evie," he said simply.

I had prepared myself for many eventualities with our transition, but I hadn't prepared for this. My mouth must've fallen open because Dawson reached over and tapped his knuckles lightly on my chin. I snapped my mouth shut; my eyes hot with tears as emotion crashed through me.

"Are you serious?" I asked, my voice thick.

He cupped my chin, his thumb swiping across my cheek and catching the tears as they fell. "Of course, I'm serious. You're the most important person in my life, and I don't want to waste any time. It's not like we rushed. We knew each other for two years before anything ever happened, and it's been a year since then. If you want to wait, I'll understand. But I just want you to know where I'm at. There is *no* doubt in my mind that I want to spend the rest of my life with you."

The thing about a man whose fallback was to tease was that when he was serious, it was breathtaking.

My own heart was going completely wild. If it could have burst into song and dance, I was certain it would've. Although I supposed the number my heart was doing on my ribs was some form of crazy tap dance.

I couldn't seem to speak, but I managed to nod and swiped a few more tears away. He never once looked away, holding my gaze the entire time.

I hiccupped. Only I could manage to get the hiccups when the only man I ever loved asked me to marry him.

"Yes," I finally whispered, joy bursting open inside.

Dawson let out a slow sigh. He closed the distance between us, catching my lips in a searing hot kiss. When he drew back, he unfolded the handkerchief with one hand and laid his palm flat. A silver band set with a sapphire sat there.

"You said it was your favorite stone," he explained when I gasped and hiccupped again.

Another thing I'd come to learn about Dawson? He remembered everything. He paid attention to the small details. We'd had a single conversation I could recall about this over dinner and drinks one evening at the lodge with friends.

I started crying all over again.

He brushed my tears away, dusting kisses over my cheeks before finding his way to my mouth again. In a matter of seconds, what started out slow evolved into a wet, open-mouthed kiss. Even though it was chilly, caught in the fire that was ever burning between us, we were tugging at each other's clothes. In a matter of minutes, Dawson had sweet-talked me out of my leggings as he wrapped his jacket around my waist while I sank down over his thick, hard length, sheathing him in my core.

A bit later while we walked back to the cabin we shared here at the lodge, Dawson held my hand warm in his. He paused at the edge of the trees, his silvery gaze catching mine in the darkness. “I love you.”

Leaning up, I ruffled his hair. “Same.”

DAWSON

Another six months later

I shouldered through the door to the back of the staff area at the lodge. I was fucking exhausted. Wade and I had done a guided hike for five days with a group. It had included white water rafting, hiking, and rock climbing. I still loved my job, but these longer trips were hard because I missed Evie when I was away.

Life was good. So good I couldn’t believe it sometimes.

Evie was in grad school for business. She still covered extra shifts at the lodge restaurant and cut her friends’ hair, but she was focused on school these days. I was hoping to see her because Dani told me she was back here doing something with Grace’s hair.

Pushing through another door from the back hallway, her voice carried to me right away, and my heart kicked up a notch. As I looked across the room, my knees buckled slightly. I didn’t think of myself as a weak man, but I was when it came to Evie.

She hadn’t seen me yet. Her glossy brown hair was pulled up in a ponytail, which swung as she moved. My eyes landed on the now obvious curve of her belly. I couldn't help the surge of pride followed immediately by lust.

She was six months pregnant, and I could hardly believe it. Also, who knew that seeing her pregnant would basically make me crazy? In the best kind of way.

Hot damn, she was so fucking sexy.

The moment I crossed the room, I was wrapping my arms around her from behind, dipping my head into her neck, and breathing in the scent of her.

She squeaked. "Oh, my God! You startled me, Dawson. Did y'all get back early?"

I lifted my head, leaning around to find a smile stretching across her face as she angled to look back at me. "Only about two hours early. I missed you."

Her cheeks flushed pretty and pink, and she leaned up to press a kiss to my cheek. "Missed you too."

Dropping my head into the sweet curve of her neck, I couldn't resist trailing a few hot, wet kisses along the silky skin there.

"Get a room," Grace protested.

Lifting my head, I ran a palm over the round curve of Evie's belly because I couldn't help myself before I stepped back. "Sorry," I said, catching Grace's eyes. "I missed Evie."

"Uh, yeah, that's kinda obvious. I'd tell her to cut my hair later, so y'all could get to it, but she's already in the middle of it," Grace explained, pointing at one side of her head, which had papers folded over sections of hair with a bright purple color bleeding through.

Evie's cheeks were still pink when she looked at me. "I'll be done in about two hours."

"I'll head home. I could seriously use a shower."

She smiled. "I was going to get pizza for dinner. Sound good?"

"Sounds perfect." I couldn't help it and had to step close just once more to press a kiss to her lips. I kept it quick, if only to prevent Grace from scolding us again.

A while later when I heard the door open, I drained my coffee and quickly rinsed the mug out in the sink. I'd been mostly abstaining when Evie was around ever since she'd gotten pregnant. I tried to be a team player and not tempt her.

Turning, I strode quickly through the archway into the living room, immediately taking the box of pizza and her bag of supplies from her arms.

"You shouldn't carry so much," I said.

She rolled her eyes. "Oh, my God. It's a box of pizza and a bag that weighs maybe a few pounds. It doesn't matter. You also don't have to sneak coffee behind my back," she added as she followed me into the kitchen.

Sliding the pizza onto the kitchen counter, I turned back and winked. "I know I don't, but I know you love your coffee, and I feel guilty whenever I have it in front of you."

She grinned. Turning, she reached to take her bag back from where I set it on the counter, but I beat her to it. "Got it. Goes in the hall closet, right?"

"You are ridiculous," she called after me.

Calling over my shoulder, I said, "Sit down and have some pizza."

When I returned to the kitchen, she had two plates out and had the refrigerator open. "What do you want to drink?"

"Just water," I replied as I reached up and got two glasses from the cabinet above the sink.

Minutes later, we were sitting at the table. Looking over at her with her lopsided ponytail, I smiled, a subtle tension unspooling inside my chest. I didn't like being away from Evie. Not at all.

It wasn't quite rational, to be honest. I knew logically speaking that she was fine on her own, but ever since she'd gotten pregnant, I found I could manufacture many, many things to worry about.

That sense of tension was an odd thing Evie had illuminated. Whenever I was with her, I enjoyed a level of comfort

I'd never experienced before. I couldn't say I had missed it before because you couldn't miss something you didn't even know existed. But she gave it to me. When I thought back to before we were together, she had always been so *easy* for me to be around.

I managed to temporarily forget my focus on her because I was fucking starving and had settled in to devour most of the pizza. After we finished eating, it was a race to beat Evie at her habit of cleaning up the kitchen. When I closed the dishwasher, I turned around to find her behind me leaning her hips against the counter opposite me.

Stepping to her, I slid my arms around her waist and buried my head in the curve of her neck. I'd never known the scent of a woman could get to me, but with Evie, it was like coming home.

"I missed you," I murmured, sliding my hand up to brush her hair away and dust kisses along the side of her neck.

She leaned back, cupping my cheek as I lifted my head. "I always miss you when you're gone."

Somehow, we went from there to a hot, messy kiss. I needed her so fiercely that before I knew it, I was shoving her skirt up around her hips and teasing the slick heat between her thighs. I savored the feel of her everywhere—the press of her belly against me, her plump breasts, and the way my heart thudded when I came inside her slick core.

A while later, we were resting on the couch with Evie on my lap. She lifted her head from my shoulder, announcing, "We have to go outside."

Considering that I was relaxed and sated with her warm on my lap, going outside was the furthest thing from my mind. "Huh? It's cold out."

She grinned. "We have a good view of Orion tonight, and it's your favorite constellation."

I could never say no to Evie, and the stars were sentimental for us. Because way back when on that rock in the darkness when I was having a bad day, Evie told me the

Little Dipper was her favorite constellation, and she never forgot that Orion was mine.

Moments later, we were on the back deck, the moon illuminating the mountains encircling Stolen Hearts Valley. "See," she said as I looked through the telescope over her shoulder. I marveled at the clarity. Evie let out a little happy sigh.

"We can do this, right?" I asked.

Every so often, the depth of what Evie represented to me, and of the family that we already had even though our little boy had yet to be born, came flying at me. Sometimes I didn't know if I could forever be the man she needed.

Leaning her head back against my shoulder and sliding her hand to curl around the nape of my neck, she murmured. "Of course, we can. It's you and me."

Thank you for reading Break My Fall - I hope you loved Dawson & Evie's story!

Up next in the Swoon Series is Truly Madly Mine. Dani and Wade have what some might call *history*. It all ended with a slushy thrown in high school.

As fate would have it, they end up working together years later. Despite Dani's best intentions, she just *might* still have a thing for Wade.

Wade just *might* do anything to get her back. When he finally gets his chance, he grabs it with both hands. Buckle up for a smoking hot second chance, friends to lovers romance!

Keep reading for a sneak peek!

Be sure to sign up for my newsletter for the latest news, teasers & more! Click here to sign up: http://jhcroixauthor.com/subscribe/

EXCERPT: TRULY MADLY MINE

Dani

My hand slipped just as I brought down a bag of flour from the shelf above me. The heavy bag bounced off another shelf and exploded, sending a cloud of flour all over me.

I opened my mouth—to provide a choice curse—only to inhale a breath of flour. A coughing and sneezing fit ensued. When I finally caught me breath, I leaned against the wall with a sigh, not even bothering to deal with the torn bag of flour on the floor.

"Bless you," a voice said from the doorway.

Fuck my life.

Opening my eyes, I glanced down to see my apron and my hands and arms dusted white. Lifting a hand, I patted my hair, sending a burst of flour into the air again. I only hoped the flour I felt on my face obscured my blush when I lifted my eyes to meet the teasing gaze of Wade Ellis.

"Thanks," I said, instantly wishing my tone didn't come out so sharp. "Remind me who's idea it was to store the flour above my head."

Wade's grin stretched wider, and my pulse—rather disobedient by the way—took off at a fast gallop. Meanwhile, a funny spinning feeling happened in my belly. There were many things I could control. The state of my body when Wade teased me was not one of them, despite my best efforts.

"Now that, I don't know. The kitchen is definitely your zone. I'm sure it was your idea."

A little laugh broke loose. Because I couldn't help it. Even if I hated that Wade happened to find me in this state, I knew he was right. I *was* bossy and didn't mind owning it. I was certain I'd had a good reason for storing the flour there, but it seemed foolish now.

"What are you doing here so early this morning anyway?" I asked, glancing around for a towel.

My eyes landed on a stack of clean dish towels just by the door, and I pushed away from the wall to reach for one.

"I'm leading a long hike today," Wade replied. "Came by to stock up on some first aid supplies."

When I lifted my hand to brush the towel over my flour-covered hair, my bracelet caught on the elastic holding my ponytail in place. "Dammit," I murmured as I moved too quickly, almost yanking the elastic out.

Wade's low chuckle send heat chasing over my skin like little licks of fire. "Hang on, let me help," he said, stepping closer.

My pulse went absolutely wild, my breath hitched in my throat and a flush of heat blasted me from head to toe. I spent a lot of time not getting too close to Wade.

All that effort was wasted. He stood right at my side, his presence intense. He exhibited an easy strength and grace no matter what he did. When I moved to try to untangle my bracelet, my elbow bumped into his muscled chest, and I almost exclaimed. Dear God, his chest was truly nothing but muscle.

My mouth did what it always did when I was around Wade and started babbling. "Geez, dude. Working out enough?" I asked, my tone sarcastic.

I felt his hands carefully untangling a few curls in the elastic around my bracelet. "You know my job keeps me in shape," he murmured in reply. The contrast of his hard body and having this massive bear of a man carefully untangling my hair made my heart squeeze a little. "There, it's going to be easiest if I just pull it out."

I lowered my arms and waited, my curls falling in a wild tangle around my shoulders as he extricated the hair band. Wade stepped back, holding up the elastic. When I took it from him, my fingers brushed against his, sending a hot jolt of electricity up my arm.

We stood there staring at each other. The normally busy staff kitchen at the lodge restaurant was quiet as dawn hadn't even arrived. It wasn't even 5:30 a.m. yet. It felt as if Wade and I were all alone in the world, caught in this little bubble. The air felt as if it were firing sparks around us.

The usual teasing look in Wade's eyes faded as he searched my face. His espresso gaze darkened. A stillness fell over me as I looked at him, letting my eyes travel over the strong, clean lines of his face. Wade was all man and tall with broad shoulders. His dark brows angled up slightly. His cheekbones were a thing of beauty—bold, sculpted curves. His perfectly straight nose was centered over his full lips. His square jaw had a shadow of stubble on it.

My fingers tingled with the urge to lift my hand and cup his cheek. I didn't know what the hell was going on with me. I couldn't seem to move. I was frozen, my breath coming in shallow little pants as I stared up at Wade. The space in the pantry was quiet for several long beats, all the while I could hear the rush of blood in my ears with every beat of my heart.

"Dani."

I heard my name on Wade's lips but it had been years since I'd heard that tone in his voice. It was rough, laced with need.

I felt caught in a current that spun into itself. The need

to finally give into what I'd been denying myself for years was so overpowering, I couldn't seem to call upon my snarky self and push back against it.

In a hot second, my head tipped back just as Wade leaned down. His lips brushed across mine when he murmured my name again, the whisper of his voice sending an electric tingle over my lips that raced through every cell in my body. I felt it course through me, sparking from the inside out.

A frayed sigh escaped. Then, Wade fit his mouth over mine. One fiery second burned into another, everything going up in flames.

This wasn't the first time I had kissed Wade. Not even close. Our young, messy kisses in high school didn't hold a candle to this one. It was quite clear Wade had some practice in the intervening years. He kissed me like he was born to it—sensual strokes of his tongue against mine, his hand lacing into my hair as he angled my head to the side and devoured my mouth.

I wasn't passive, oh no. I wanted this too much. Denial might've work for a while—hell, even for years—but once the gates fell, all hell broke loose.

I was lost in the kiss, the feeling of his strong, hard body holding mine against his, and the taste of him was intoxicating. Sweet Jesus, his kisses had set me on fire inside and out.

"Hey Dani, do you—" The question stopped abruptly. "Oh! Oh my!"

The sound of footsteps hurrying away from the pantry echoed as Wade and I broke apart, our breath coming in sharp heaves.

We stared at each other. Oh my God.

Coming December 2019!

Truly Madly Mine

. . .

If you love steamy, small town romance, take a visit to Willow Brook, Alaska in my Into The Fire Series. Check out Burn For Me - a second chance romance for the ages. It's FREE on all retailers! Don't miss Cade & Amelia's story!

Go here to sign up for information on new releases: http://jhcroixauthor.com/subscribe/

FIND MY BOOKS

Thank you for reading Break My Fall! I hope you enjoyed the story. If so, you can help other readers find my books in a variety of ways.

1) Write a review!
2) Sign up for my newsletter, so you can receive information about upcoming new releases & receive a FREE copy of one of my books: http://jhcroixauthor.com/subscribe/
3) Like and follow my Amazon Author page at https://amazon.com/author/jhcroix
4) Follow me on Bookbub at https://www.bookbub.com/authors/j-h-croix
5) Follow me on Twitter at https://twitter.com/JHCroix
6) Like my Facebook page at https://www.facebook.com/jhcroix

Swoon Series

This Crazy Love
Wait For Me
Break My Fall
Truly Madly Mine - coming December 17th, 2019!

Into The Fire Series

Burn For Me
Slow Burn
Burn So Bad
Hot Mess
Burn So Good
Sweet Fire
Play With Fire
Melt With You
Burn For You
Crash & Burn

Brit Boys Sports Romance

The Play
Big Win
Out Of Bounds
Play Me
Naughty Wish

Diamond Creek Alaska Novels

When Love Comes
Follow Love
Love Unbroken
Love Untamed
Tumble Into Love
Christmas Nights

Last Frontier Lodge Novels

Take Me Home
Love at Last
Just This Once
Falling Fast
Stay With Me
When We Fall
Hold Me Close

Crazy For You

Just Us

Catamount Lion Shifters

Protected Mate

Chosen Mate

Fated Mate

Destined Mate

A Catamount Christmas

Ghost Cat Shifters

The Lion Within

Lion Lost & Found

ACKNOWLEDGMENTS

I'll start where it matters - my readers! Maybe I say it with every book, but your support means so freaking much. A giant hug to all of you!

My editor keeps me on point, and I am so grateful. Much appreciation to Terri D. for scouring every sentence to catch my mistakes.

Janine, Beth P., Terri E., Heather H., & Carolyne B. - thank you every time for finding the last minute details.

My husband cheers on every book and supports me even when my imaginary worlds take up a lot of time.

My dogs are my furry support team and spend most of their time somewhere nearby when I'm writing.

xoxo

J.H. Croix

ABOUT THE AUTHOR

USA Today Bestselling Author J. H. Croix lives in a small town in the historical farmlands of Maine with her husband and two spoiled dogs. Croix writes contemporary romance with sassy women and alpha men who aren't afraid to show some emotion. Her love for quirky small-towns and the characters that inhabit them shines through in her writing. Take a walk on the wild side of romance with her bestselling novels!

Places you can find me:
jhcroixauthor.com
jhcroix@jhcroix.com

facebook.com/jhcroix
twitter.com/jhcroix
instagram.com/jhcroix

Made in the USA
Monee, IL
09 March 2020

22949891R00132